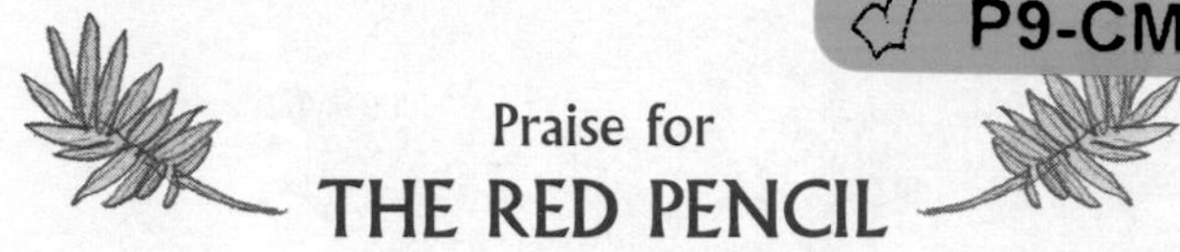

Praise for

THE RED PENCIL

★ "Amira's thoughts and drawings are **vividly brought to life** through Pinkney's lyrical verse and Evans's lucid line illustrations, which infuse the narrative with emotional intensity. . . . **An essential purchase.**" —*School Library Journal* (starred review)

★ "Pinkney uses **deft strokes** to create engaging characters through the poetry of their observations and the poignancy of their circumstances. . . . **A soulful story** that captures the magic of possibility, even in difficult times." —*Kirkus Reviews* (starred review)

★ "Pinkney faces war's horrors head on, yet also conveys a sense of **hope and promise.**"
—*Publishers Weekly* (starred review)

★ "[If] the **evocative poetry** is the novel's beating heart, Evans' spare, open, **graceful line drawings** are its breath. . . . Ultimately, this is an inspirational story of the harrowing adversity countless children face, the **resilience** with which they meet it, and the **inestimable power** of imagination and learning to carry them through." —*Booklist* (starred review)

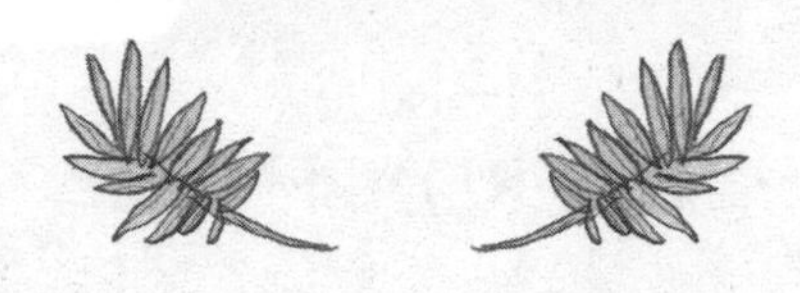

"This book **whispers into the reader's heart.**"
—KAREN HESSE,
Newbery Medal–winning author of *Out of the Dust*

"The **perfect marriage of lyrical text and evocative drawings,** *The Red Pencil* demonstrates the transformative power of artistic expression—even in the worst of times. **Haunting, eye-opening, and deeply inspiring.**"
—PATRICIA McCORMICK,
National Book Award finalist for *Never Fall Down* and *Sold*

A *New York Times* Editors' Choice
A Junior Library Guild Selection
A *School Library Journal* Best Book of the Year
A *Kirkus Reviews* Best Book of the Year
A *New York Times* Notable Book
An ALSC Notable Children's Book
A Children's Africana Book Award Winner
An NAACP Image Award Nominee
A Center for the Study of Multicultural Children's Literature Best Multicultural Book
A Kids' Indie Next List Pick

THE RED PENCIL

THE RED PENCIL

BY ANDREA DAVIS PINKNEY

ILLUSTRATED BY SHANE W. EVANS

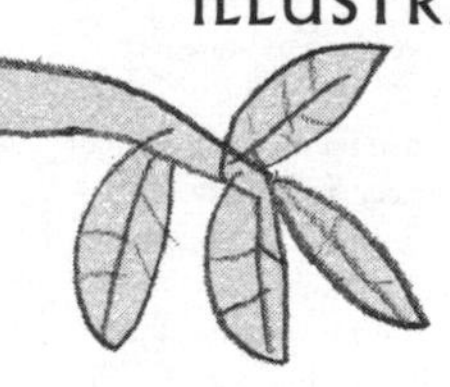

LITTLE, BROWN AND COMPANY
NEW YORK BOSTON

Little, Brown and Company

Hachette Book Group
1290 Avenue of the Americas, New York, NY 10104
Visit us at lb-kids.com

Little, Brown and Company is a division of Hachette Book Group, Inc.
The Little, Brown name and logo are trademarks of Hachette Book Group, Inc.

The publisher is not responsible for websites (or their content) that are not owned by the publisher.

First Paperback Edition: November 2015
First published in hardcover in September 2014 by Little, Brown and Company

Library of Congress Cataloging-in-Publication Data

Pinkney, Andrea Davis, author.
The red pencil / by Andrea Davis Pinkney ; illustrated by Shane Evans.—First edition.
pages cm
Summary: "After her tribal village is attacked by militants, Amira, a young Sudanese girl, must flee to safety at a refugee camp, where she finds hope and the chance to pursue an education in the form of a single red pencil and the friendship and encouragement of a wise elder"— Provided by publisher.
ISBN 978-0-316-24780-1 (hardcover : alk. paper)—ISBN 978-0-316-24782-5 (paperback)—
ISBN 978-0-316-24781-8 (ebook)—ISBN 978-0-316-37154-4 (library edition ebook)
[1. Novels in verse. 2. Blacks—Sudan—Fiction.
3. Refugees—Fiction. 4. Sudan—Fiction.] I. Evans, Shane, illustrator. II. Title.
PZ7.5.P56Re 2014 [Fic]—dc23 2013044753

10 9 8 7

LSC-C

Printed in the United States of America

To HP, who showed me the pencil.
—AP

Thank you, God, for this gift. I dedicate
this book to the children at St. Mary
Kevin Orphanage Motherhood in
the small town of Kajjansi, Uganda.
These brave children have shown me
resounding Joy.
—SWE

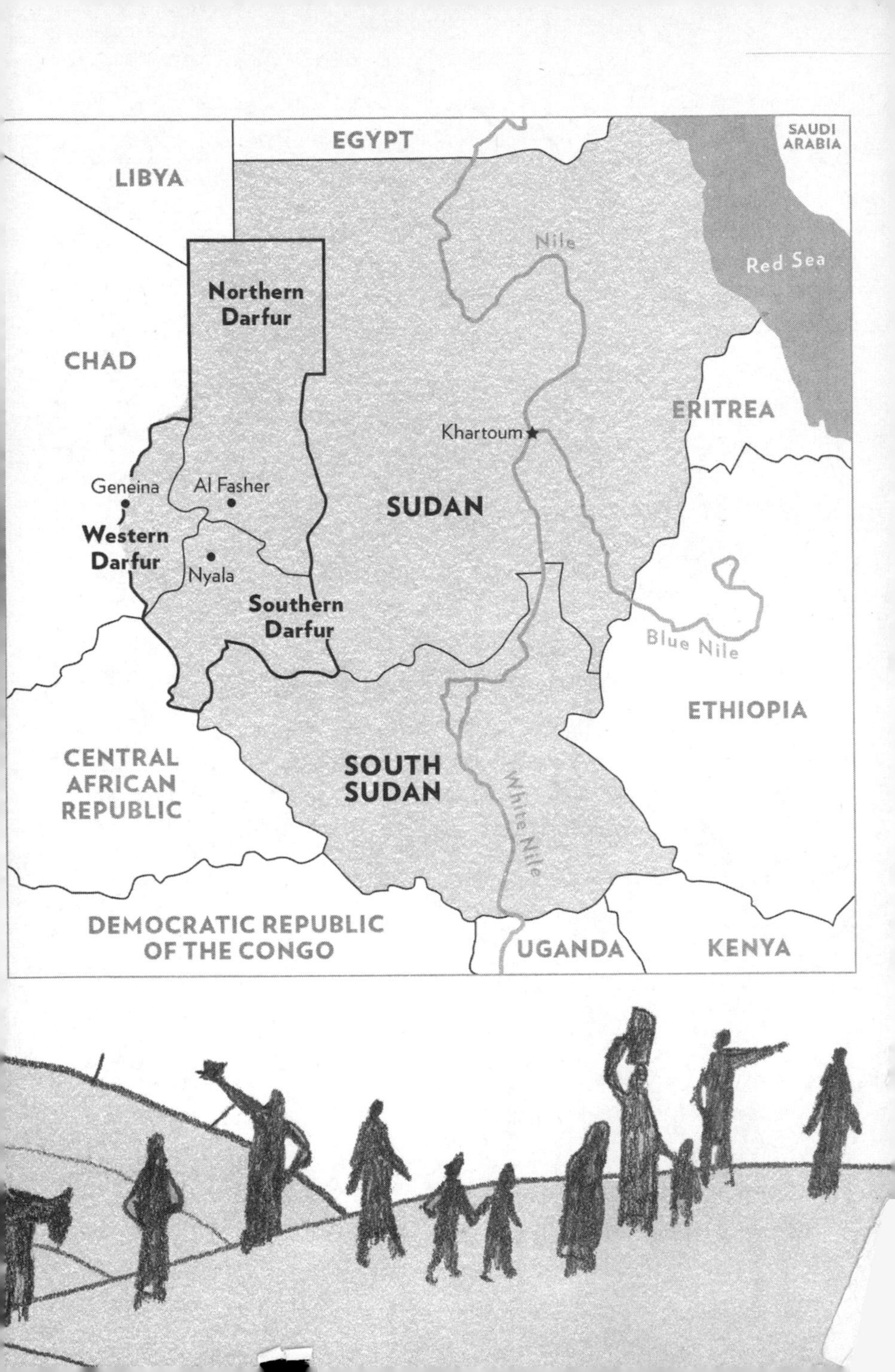
EGYPT
SAUDI ARABIA
LIBYA
Nile
Red Sea
Northern Darfur
CHAD
ERITREA
Khartoum
Geneina
Al Fasher
SUDAN
Western Darfur
Nyala
Southern Darfur
Blue Nile
ETHIOPIA
CENTRAL AFRICAN REPUBLIC
SOUTH SUDAN
White Nile
DEMOCRATIC REPUBLIC OF THE CONGO
UGANDA
KENYA

PART 1

OUR FARM

South Darfur, Africa

September 2003–March 2004

WHEAT

Finally, I am twelve.
Old enough to wear a *toob.*

As soon as I wake,
Muma whispers a birthday wish.

"Blessings for all the years to come, Amira."

My mother has been awake for hours,
starting early with farm chores.

On this birthday morning
bright
as the sun's first yawn,
ripened wheat
sways.

Its golden braids
are woven with the promise
of a hearty harvest.

Ya, wheat!

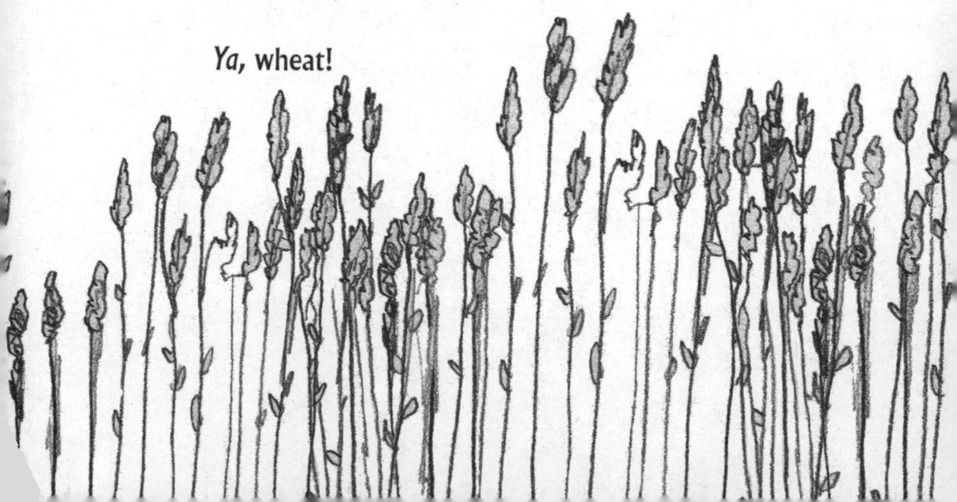

Our greatest crop.

Our gleaming pride,
stretching tall,
glinting beneath the sun's smile.

Ya, wheat!

You will make
flour,
loaves,
golden cake.

Ya, wheat—such abundance!

Our village glistens,
greets me
with a wink that shines bright
on this new day.

On my new year.

DANDO'S DELIGHT

As this special morning stirs,
I watch
a sparrow.

She juts
from the wheat's strands,
rustling.

Dando runs up from behind,
scoops me into strong arms,
folded loaves,
inviting me to ride.

"Come, girl child, fly!"

I squeal.
"Dando!
I'm now too old and too big
for this little-girl game!"

"Amira Bright,
it is true that you are taller,
but you are never too old
to greet the sky.
Up, up, girl!"

He swings me,
long legs,
okra-toed feet,
dusty,
flailing.

High up,
delighting.

"Show the other birds
how precious you are,
Amira Bright!"

My insides flip-flop.

Dando shouts,
as if proclaiming a great truth:

"Amira Bright—*yaaaa!*
Girl child, rising."

In Dando's arms,
I *can* fly.

In Dando's arms,
I *am* bright.

Up, up so high.
All of me.

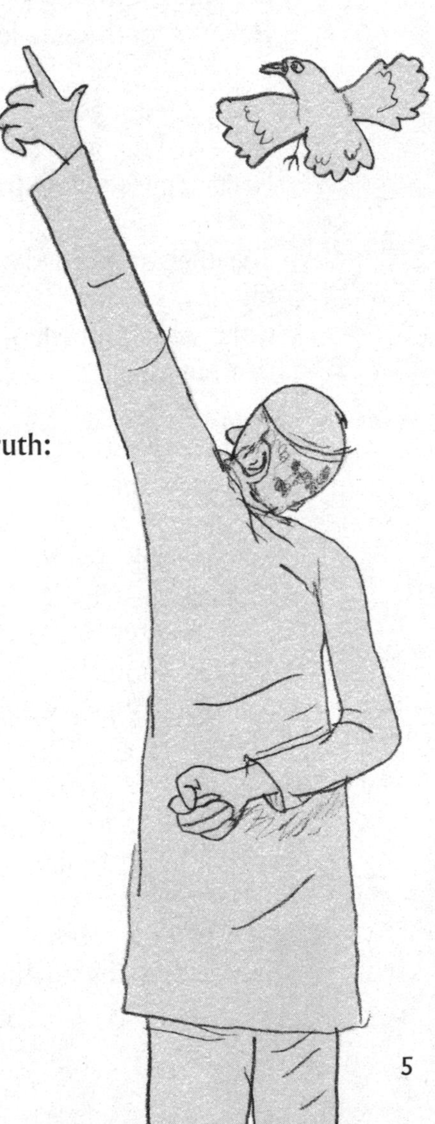

LOST TOOTH

When we were six,
and small,
and filled with silly giggles,
Halima's tooth came loose.

She wanted it gone.
She asked me to help.
Halima, my so-close friend.

Together we wiggled and tugged
the tiny,
wobbly speck of white
that hung tight.

That tooth was stubborn.
It wouldn't give.

Halima yanked at it.
So hard, she tried.

Oh, that tooth!
A little bitty pest with a mighty will.

One day,
I told Halima to open her mouth
as wide as a yawning hyena's.

I pinched the tooth
between my thumb and biggest finger.

Bent back that baby thing,
jerked it—*pop!*

Halima's tooth flew from her,
landed in the sand.

We sifted through cream-colored grains,
searching.

But it was truly gone.
Halima said, "*Aakh*—that hurt!"

I said,
"Yes, but you are free of it, Halima.
It's time to be happy!"

DIZZY DONKEY

"Let's play dizzy donkey,"
Halima said.

We faced each other,
fingers laced—and we spun!

Heads back,
noses up.

Whirling girls
together.

Twirling,
giggly-tipping,
sideways sky,
tummies churning,
turning us
into
dizzy donkeys.

OPPORTUNITY

I thought silly giggles
and dizzy donkey
would always be.

But today
Halima and I
must say good-bye.

Her father is determined
to find something more.

I hear him tell Dando
he wants to go from small to big,
from village to city.

He's looking for something he calls
Opportunity.

Halima's father no longer wants to sell his wares
at our small weekly village market.

He's eager to meet customers
in Nyala's bustling bazaar.

Patrons who,
every day,
will pay
higher prices
for his salt, sugar, coffee, and corn.

He wants to live among lively people,
and cars
and things fast and shiny.

And,
Halima's father,
he's always mumbling something
about leaving before it's too late.

Halima's mother, a weaver,
is excited
to show off
her patterned fabrics
to city women and wealthy foreign visitors
with big wallets.

Words flap from her
like giddy chickens escaping their pen.

She is so squawky, that woman.
Especially when she talks about life in the city.

Today I wonder
if Halima's mother
has wing feathers
hiding beneath her *toob.*

SCHOOL

Halima tells me
that with the money her parents earn
they will be able to afford to send her
to Gad Primary School,
on the outskirts of Nyala,
Darfur's largest town.

There's word in our village about Gad.
Much of it scorn.
Some, praise.

Talk of Gad is a burlap sack
of mixed opinions.

Gad is a school that welcomes girls.
Gad pushes past tradition.
I want to go to Gad.

I've never seen that school.
I know of it only through village rumblings.

Whenever Halima speaks of Nyala
and of Gad,
I am reminded that she is truly the child
of her mother,
flap-flapping with excitement
about her new city home and school.

My friend's parents are modern people,
not stifled by tradition.

Most others in our village
are nothing like Halima's mother and father.

Most are as closed-minded as donkeys
who will not turn their eyes to see anything
beyond what is right in front of them.

Most are small, not big, in their thinking.

This is especially true of Muma.
When it comes to schooling,
my mother is the most tight-minded of anyone.

She does not like the idea of Gad,
or any place where girls learn
to read
or write,
in Arabic or English,
or think beyond a life
of farm chores and marriage.

Muma,
born into a flock of women,
locked in a hut of tradition.

That hut.
A closed-off place
with no windows for letting in fresh ideas.

Sometimes I want to ask,
"Muma, can you breathe?"

PINCHED

This morning,
Halima's family has loaded their oxen
with everything they own.

Tin pots.
Grain buckets.
Sleeping straw.
Firewood.

Saying good-bye to my
so-close friend hurts
worse
than yanking a tooth.

When her oxen's hind parts
become a rippling blur on the horizon,
I'm pinched
by two feelings at once.

Aakh—
I will miss my so-close friend.

Aakh—
I do not like being left behind.

I wish *I* were the one
leaving our village,
going from small to big,
searching for something called
Opportunity.

From inside me comes a tug—*pop!*—

I cry.

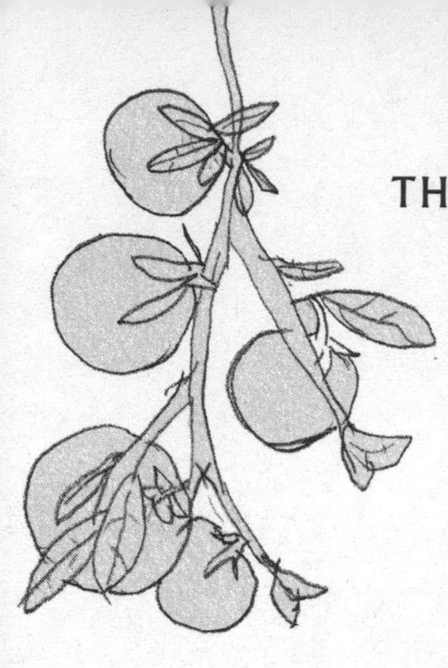

THE WAGER

Dando and Old Anwar
have made a bet.

Who can grow
the most tomatoes
by picking time?

"My fruits are always
more plentiful
than yours," says Old Anwar.

Dando would brag
about his tomatoes
all day
if he didn't have other work to do.

"Your tomatoes
are green knots of nothing.
You may have
more, but it is more of what is paltry.
My tomatoes *are* more.
More plump.
More beautiful."

Old Anwar says,
"Proud man, it is ugly to be so boastful."

My father's hands rest firmly at his hips.
He's having fun ridiculing Old Anwar.

"Your little green rocks, struggling on their vines.
You believe they are tomatoes.
I believe they will crack the teeth
of anyone who dares to bite into them.
How do you expect to feed people
with those gnarly things?"

Dando won't stop.

"You should use what you are calling tomatoes
as washing stones
to pound stains from your clothes."

Old Anwar is wearing a gray *jallabiya.*
He waves his fist,
right up to Dando's face. *"Bah!"*

Dando leans hard toward Old Anwar.
He scowls.
"*Bah* to you and your lumpy tomatoes!"

Old Anwar stomps off,
dust rising
from his sandals.

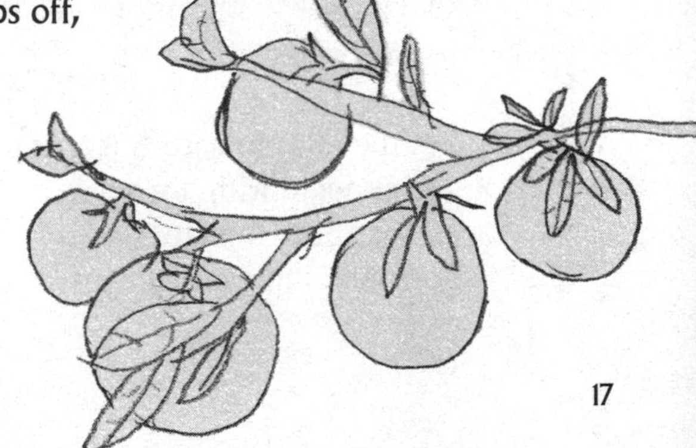

FRUITLESS

Why do grown-up men argue about such silly things?
Tomatoes don't care
which ones in their group are green or gnarly,
or small,
or red or plump.

They're just fruits.
They don't know anything
about being ugly or pretty.

Old Anwar and Dando,
friends who have fun arguing.

Old Anwar has been our neighbor
for my whole life.

But then this tomato wager started,
and brought with it a war.
A war about tomatoes!
So dumb, this tomato fight.

CONTEST

In the evening before I sleep,
Dando comes to my pallet.

"Dream of good things, Amira Bright," he says.

I ask,
"Why do you and Old Anwar fight about fruits?"

Dando tries to reason with me,
but he is not convincing.

"We are not fighting. We are having a contest."

WAR

My father tries to explain something
that is more twisted
than a tangled
skein of raggedy thread.
"Amira, we are living in a time of war."

I've heard the elders talk of this.
But Dando is doing more than talking.
He is telling.

I listen.

Like a mangled mess,
Dando's words are
hard to follow.

I can make no sense
of anything he says.

He uses strange terms:
Persecution
Rebellion
Genocide

I understand a little more
when Dando explains,
"There has been fighting for land."

I say,
"It's senseless
to fight over something
Allah has made for everyone."

Dando nods.
"That is only part of the reason
for this war."

My father chooses words
as if he is carefully selecting only
the most primed tomatoes.

"Brothers are killing each other
over the belief
that in the Almighty's eyes
some people are superior."

Dando's words:

Twisted

Tangled

Raggedy

Knotted

Nonsense

AS I SEE IT

Harder I listen,
still trying to piece together
this nonsense puzzle.

I say it as I see it:
"This war you tell me about,
it is like the battles
between you and Old Anwar."

Dando flinches.

I say it as I see it:
"Fighting about tomatoes is such
foolishness!"

Dando is quick to dismiss
my reasoning.

"Amira, my bright daughter,
Old Anwar and I are not at war."

I say it as I see it:
"You are."

CHORES

There's a bad part
about turning twelve.

In the eyes of my family,
I'm nearly a grown-up.

This means
I must work even harder at farm chores.

Muma says
I'm to accept these duties with grace and obedience,
and not a speck of complaint.

And so, I do.
Daily, I do.

I haul
sacks of grain
from our storage hut
to the animal corral.

I weed
every coarse,
thick-rooted shoot
that chokes our
leafy greens.

I husk
corn and millet,

and anything with a hull
that needs my nimble fingers
to remove its shell.

I peel
potatoes, onions, pumpkins, squash.

I chop-chop-chop
all of these
for making them sing in a pot.

And now, since I'm
nearly grown,
I have a new chore—
raking cow plop
to spread at the base of our crops.

This special duty
has brought me happy friends—
flies who like to cluster
on the freshly gathered,
still-moist mounds.

I wish
our cows
didn't eat so much grass.

I wish
our ample animals
would give me less to work with.

BIRTH STORY

When Dando tells of my birth,
he smiles as wide as a moon's crescent.

"Amira Bright," he begins,
"you came ahead of the dawn,
before sunlight cracked open the dark.
Before it could spread thick
above the tomato garden."

Each year, in the days following my birthday,
my father shares this tale.
He tells it
with so much joy.

"Your mother, she had risen early, Amira,
to pick the okra. To save it from the day's heat."

Muma says, "The sun, she has a blistering palm.
If I wake before she does,
my gathering is easier."

I nod. I know.

Muma keeps the story's thread strong,
pulling it
with hands that dance,
as she tells more.

"You came so fast,
before the day was to break.
Hurling ahead, quick as the winds."

HEARTBEAT

My birth story:
    Close, close.
    Beating-heart close.

A story so much a part of me.

    Like my fence-post legs,
    a part of me.

    Like my braids,
    knitted and twisty,
    a part of me.

Close as my skin, this story is.

    I know every inch,
    from its ear tips to its tail.
    I know its in-between places, too.

Close as my breathing, this story is.

    Close, close.
    Beating-heart close.
    My birth story.

OKRA

My birth story has funny pieces.
Dando takes pride in telling them.
Muma adds the silliest bit—the okra.

"I was gathering
from the far-off fields
when you began to press from my insides,
pushing to be born, Amira."

Dando is quick to speak.
"Your mother,
arms filled
with okra shoots, started to run
toward our hut."

Muma always is laughing at this part of the story.
"I was balancing okra in the folds of my *toob*,
and, you, Amira,
in my belly.

"But that okra, and you,
came tumbling from me!"

Dando says,
"Muma was a stuffed barrel,
bobbling across the land,
okra dropping."

Dando wipes the wet from his eyes,
tears brought on by hard laughing.
"I called, 'Stop running, wife!'"

"Did she stop?" I ask,
already knowing what comes next.

"Your mother, she never stops her running."
Muma says, "I *did* slow down."

Dando and I say,
"To pick up the okra!"

Muma huffs.

All of us, together sing:
"Not good to waste okra!"

TWIG

Dando slips it out from behind him.
It's something he knows I will truly love.

My father has brought me a sturdy twig.
A new one, sharp at its tip.
More pointy than the twig I have now.

He says,
"For making your sand pictures, Amira Bright."

I touch my finger to my gift's angled end.

I say,
"This will be my turning-twelve twig."

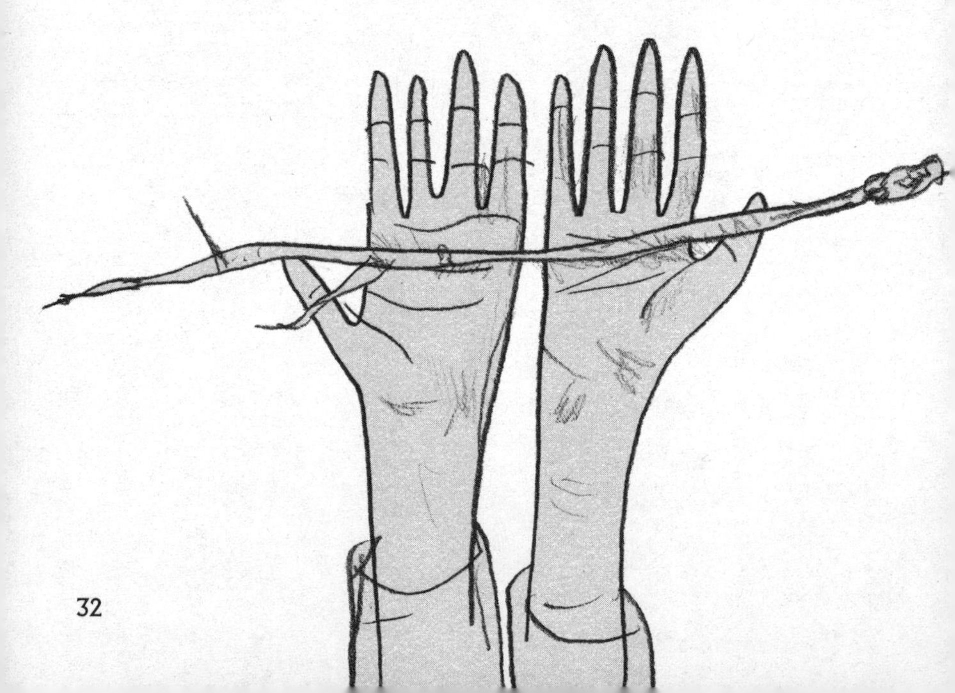

DITTY

Leila pouts.
My little sister
wants it to be *her* birthday.

She wants to trade her *tarha*
for my *toob.*

"In time," Muma says.
"You have only seen four years.
When you are Amira's age,
we will dress you in bright cottons."

Leila is disappointed,
yet she has her own gift for me.

She sings me a ditty:

"Your turning-twelve twig—
big!

Your turning-twelve twig—
long!

Your turning-twelve twig—
thick!

Your turning-twelve twig—
strong!"

WAKING THE MOON

When the moon winks,
then waves good-bye,
it is a bad sign.

A hiding moon is a curse.

It means
the worst
luck is sure to fall.

If a curtain of clouds
closes
on a swelling moon's smile,
we have reason to frown.

That is why we wake the moon.

Tradition tells us
to make the waking *loud*.
To rouse that moon.
To scare it out,
to full sight.

I grab a pan.
I beat,
beat,
beeeeeat.

Dando rolls two drums
to right outside our house.

To where he thinks
the moon might appear.

He smacks at his drum's taut skin,
slow at first.

Then *slams!*

Pumps his drums
in mad-wild pounding.

Bam-bam!
Bam-bam!

Muma has made
an ox-bell belt for calling the moon.

She doesn't *wear* the belt.
She *waves* it.

Shakes it.
Rattles its rhythms.

Leila, she just shouts.
"Come, moon—out!"

GLOWING SAYIDDA

There are nights when the moon
wastes no time.

She surrenders to our call.
Shows her waxing white.
Stays.

But sometimes, *Sayidda* Moon,
a glowing lady,
will not cooperate.

That milk-bellied lady
refuses to reveal herself.

When she gets willful,
I wonder:

Is she up there laughing
at our ways?

Then there are nights like this one
when that moon is a trickster.

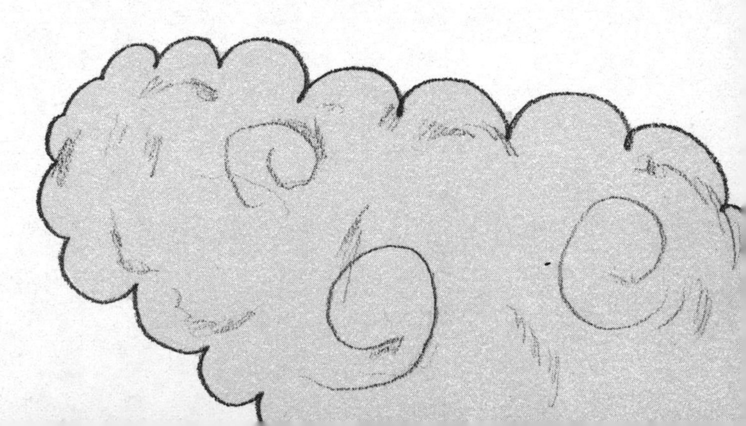

She peeks,
then hides,
forcing us to guess
if we need
to keep up
with the ox bell,
the drumbeat,
the shout-out-loud
call
that will bring her into view
until sunrise announces
night's farewell.

LEILA

Little Leila fought her way into this world.
She was born on a night
when the moon had tucked itself
into the sky's deepest pockets.

This was our first knowing
that my sister would somehow be different.

With Muma birthing Leila,
our villagers called for the moon,
louder than ever.
They wanted to keep curses away from the baby.

The thundering of their drums and pans
pummeled the night's thick blackness.

But *Sayidda* Moon,
she stayed hidden.
She couldn't be summoned,
no matter how hard we tried.

This was not good, and Dando knew it.
So did I.
Muma, too.
Dando flung shouts
and whoops
toward the sky.

I helped.
I hollered.
I beat Muma's tin cooking kettle
with every bit of strength in my small hands.

Like me, Leila came quickly.
Muma crouched, and there she was.

"Birthing Leila was fast, but not easy.
A beautiful baby, but scrawny,"
Muma remembers.

"Sharp elbows,
pointed knees,
bony heels,
flat feet,
and a hard head."

Dando always says,
"Leila, a delicate jewel."

OUR BENT BABY

My sister was born hardly breathing,
nearly blue.

Dando swabbed the insides
of her mouth with two fingers.
He sucked at her nose holes
to release the mucous plugs
that kept air out.

When Leila took her first breath,
it was a weak one,
a soundless cry.

The first thing I noticed
were Leila's bowed legs.
One of them so misshapen,
so sickled.
Half a limb with a tiny foot at the end,
toes sewn together.

The other leg, and both Leila's arms,
were oddly shaped,
like pods on a tamarind tree.

My sister's spine was bent.
A crooked,
hooked back
on a baby.

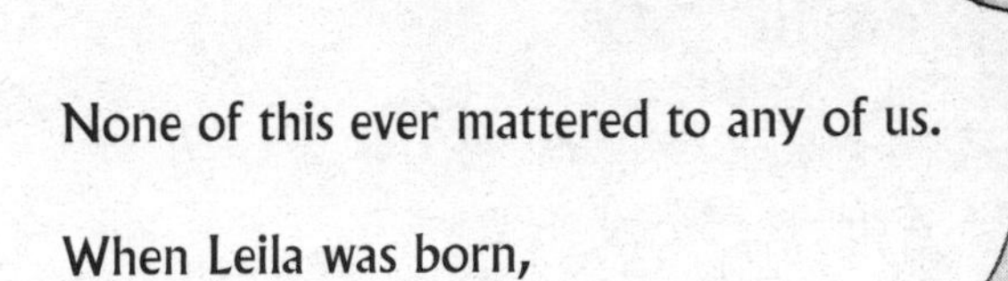

None of this ever mattered to any of us.

When Leila was born,
Muma held her gently.

Dando embraced them both,
his arms a cloak,
protecting.

He said, "This baby will keep us all strong.
That is the way of a child who comes
with so much specialness.
We will stretch to meet her."

Little Leila,
loved.

DOUBLE JOY

Nali was born on the same night as Leila.

Farha, our sheep,
moaned once,
long,
and Nali slid from her.

On that night Dando said,
"A girl and a lamb, born under the same sky.
That is double joy."

Dando had come from Farha's pen,
rushing to tell me and Muma we'd been blessed with a lamb
to go along with my baby sister.

He said,
"Leila and the lamb, each of them treasures."

That's when Leila's half cry
turned to a sudden squeal.

That's when Leila named our
just-birthed lamb.

Oh, did she wail!

"Naaaaalleee...Naaaaallleee...Naaaallllеее!"

Muma lifted both palms facing heaven,
rejoicing at the loud newborn's sound.

"Such beautiful, strong music," she said.

This is how Farha's lamb got her name:

Nali.

It was like having two sisters at the same time.
Two babies to love.

Double joy.

GAMAL

From the beginning,
Leila was a frail child.

But as she grew,
her stunted limbs
and hunched backbone
got strong.

Walking was a struggle.
My sister mostly hobbled.

Then one day
Leila met Gamal,
a spirited village boy her same age.

Gamal,
sometimes filled with the wind's mischief.
Other times, wise for a child.

GOAL

Leila has always worked hard
to keep up with Gamal.

There are days when Gamal helps Leila.
And there are days
when he niggles with her.

Gamal has shown Leila
how to play soccer with a tin can
that is more bent than she is.

When they first started to play,
Gamal taught Leila to use her stumpy feet
to make their squashed-in can pop
through tall grass,
and bounce over dunes.

Leila isn't fast,
but she's determined.

Old Anwar crafted crutches for Leila,
two sturdy,
sanded branches.

My bent baby sister took the crutches,
but refused to use them.

Since then,
there have been many days
when Leila and Gamal are squabbling,
racing,
bumping
to get their bent-up tin can
past these two weighty branches,
jammed in the sand,
now standing proud,
serving as goalposts.

TRADITION HUT

Muma and I talk easily about most things:
    How best to stack kindling.
    When sugarcane is ready to harvest.
    Ways to peel potatoes.

But there is one thing Muma will not allow me
to address with her—school.

Since Halima left,
I've brought it up quietly,
but before I can get my words out,
Muma slaps them away like flies.

When I dare speak
of my thirst
for books
and writing,
and the discovery of numbers,
Muma scolds me with her eyes.

"Schooling costs money we do not have," she says.
"What they teach from those books
is useless to you, Amira.
We need you here, to milk our cows,
to pick okra and melons,
to rake."

I do not like hearing this.
I do not like what I know Muma will say next.

"Someday,
when you marry,
you will not need to read.
A good wife lets her husband do the reading."

No!
Not one bit do I like this.

"What if I never marry?" I huff.
Muma says, "Do not speak so foolishly."

Muma's snarled thinking.
It's so backward!

CHASING THE WIND

Like Old Anwar's donkey,
I tug
at why it would be good
to attend classes at Gad Primary School.

I persist,
pulling hard on my desire.

"Muma," I say,
"I can help make our farm better
if I know how to read.
Books can tell us good ways
to grow more wheat and beans,
and corn, and okra."

Muma's face is tight.
Can she tell I'm being dishonest?

The truth of it is simple:
I want to go to school to learn about things
other than beans and okra and animal plop.

Muma is stern when she says,
"Your desire to read is a waste of time, Amira.
It serves no purpose."

A mother can challenge her child's words,
but the reverse isn't allowed.

I can't help it, though.

I ask,
"What about Halima and her family?
They are discovering new things."

Muma says,
"Those people are chasing the wind."

GOZ

Sprinkled by Allah
from fingertips
quick to spread sand
as far as we can see.

There it is.
And *there* it is.
And *there,* too.
And here.
And everywhere.

Soft sand.
Oh, this *goz.*
So much of it!

Between our toes.
In our clothes.
Through our hair.
Up our noses.

Draping its gritty mix
over our land.
Goz.
Darfur's great soil blanket.

Much good comes from *goz.*
From *goz,* Dando's tomatoes grow.
Through *goz,* melon heads poke.

Nali sleeps
on soft sheets
of newly blown *goz*.

In *goz*,
goats,
donkeys,
cows,
they rest.

In *goz*,
I belong.

Goz is my place to be.
I'm at home in so much sand.

Ya, goz.
Where my new twig
and I
wander, wander, wander.

Fly.

        Dream.

Shape.
        Swirl.
Make.
        Me.
Free.

DRAWING

Sand folds in on itself when it's been poked.
That's why I sharpen my twig's end
before I begin—
to pierce the sand.

To strike my lines.
To draw.

First, I jab at the sand's surface.
I plunge my twig's point,
splitting open warm, brown powder,
making it obey.

Then I *pull* back
in a single quick-strike
that forms an arc,
sloping *long*.

I like this line.
I draw a second one
to mirror the first.

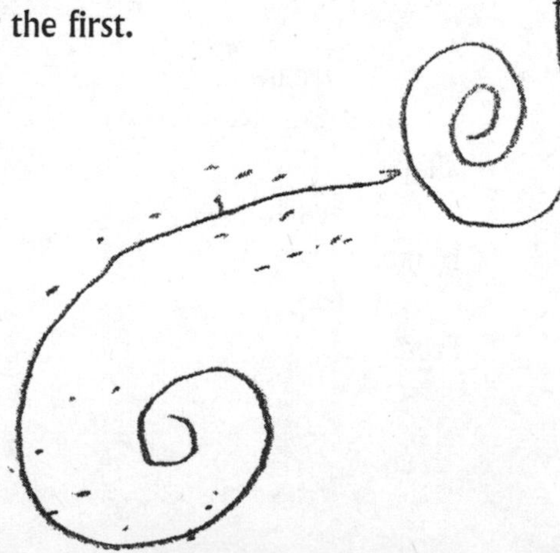

These side-by-side swerves
reveal a bird,
wings wide.
Soaring
from my twig's tip.

Created with my own hands.

Drawing, drawing
in the sand.

HAND, TWIG, SPARROW

When I draw, it's not me doing it.
It's my hand.
And my twig.
And my *sparrow.*

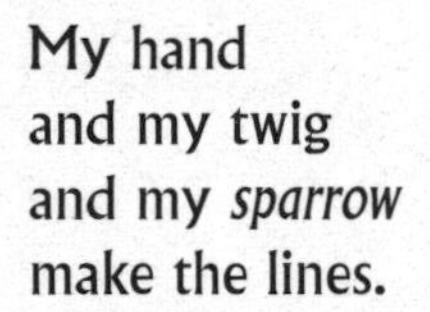

My hand
and my twig
and my *sparrow*
make the lines.

My hand
and my twig
and my *sparrow*
do the dance
on the sand.

I never know
what my hand
and my twig
and my *sparrow*
will create.

My hand
holds my twig.

But my twig goes
on its own.

My *sparrow*—that's what's inside me:

flight.

THE JANJAWEED

My mother doesn't want me to go to school,
yet I must endure
today's lesson from Muma
about something called the Janjaweed.

I've heard grown-ups speak of this,
but only with other grown-ups.

Now Muma is speaking to me.
Quietly.
Clearly.
She watches my eyes
to make sure I'm paying attention.

Muma tells me
the Janjaweed
have formed as the result
of this war Dando has tried to explain.

"The Janjaweed are bad people," Muma says.

I know what *bad people* means,
but Muma soon turns this
into a difficult lesson.

Like my father making no sense
of war,
my mother uses strange words
to help me understand.

These words do no good
in teaching me:

Armed
Militia
Bandits
Renegades

Muma says *Janjaweed*
means
"devils on horseback."

I try to pay attention,
but I'm struggling.

FRIGHT

I work hard
to find meaning
in what sounds like
a tale for
telling at night,
when we want to scare each other.

I listen,
only out of respect
for Muma,
and because,
when my strong mother speaks
of the Janjaweed,
her whole face fills with fright.

I fidget.
I want this lesson over.

Muma collects both my hands in hers.
She holds firm.
"Amira, look at me," she insists.

I make myself stay with her gaze.

My mother says,
"The Janjaweed attack without warning.
If ever they come—run."

POSSIBILITIES

Dando and I have a favorite game called
What Else Is Possible?

The only real rule for our game
is that answers to the question
What else is possible?
can only be good.

Dando goes first.

"If you wake to find your sandals gone, do you worry?"
Dando answers his own question.
This is how the game works.

He says,
"Worrying, that is a waste of time.
Better to ask, 'What *else* is possible?'"

Dando peels off his own sandal, waves it.

He insists, "Your sandals may not be gone at all,
only missing, while a generous hand mends
their worn edges."

Now it's my turn.
"If two days pass, then five, then seven,
and still no sandals, do you worry?"

I shake my head fast, ready to answer.

I tell Dando,
"It *could* be those generous mending hands
have stitched you a whole new pair of sandals."

"Made of gold!" Dando adds.
Dando waves both his sandals.

I wave my sandals, too,
one right, one left.

"Lift them high," Dando says. "High!
They are new, and glistening, our sandals."

What Else Is Possible?
is a game about looking at things
in shiny ways.

LINES

I never know
where my drawings will go.

My twig tells me.
My twig leads.

I follow
by watching my twig
decide.

I'm only the holder
of the instrument that makes
picture-music
on our parched land.

My twig takes over.

The up-and-down lines
grow longer.

Are those camel legs?

The body of a tree?

Muma's arms stretched,
praising?

I add a top to the lines.

Could this be
our square-shaped
home?

Maybe it's the lane
where our clay house sits?

"Twig," I say,
"show me."

That's the mystery,
the happy surprise,
of turning the sand's surface
into something new
to view.

AGREEING

Dando and Old Anwar agree
on me.

I am raking plop.
I will do anything to stall this chore.
So I do something I should *not* do.
I pretend to be working hard so I can
        listen.

Behind the stall fence,
seeing through its slats.
        A good view.

It's not right to listen
when my ears haven't been invited.

But my ears can't help it.
They're doing what ears are meant to do.

Old Anwar and Dando parcel hay,
        gather grain.

Old Anwar says, "Amira is a special child."

"You are right," says Dando.
"My daughter has a glint about her."

Old Anwar tosses corn pellets.

Our chickens flock,
collect,
peck,
take.

"Amira gets her glimmer from you,"
Old Anwar says.

To hear better, I stop raking.

Our chickens, are they listening, too?

Old Anwar asks Dando,
"Do you remember your boyhood?
You were filled with such curiosity.
A story-lover."

"I *do* remember," Dando says.

Old Anwar asks,
"Do you recall who taught you to read?"

Dando bows,
showing Old Anwar his respect.
"I was Amira's age."

Old Anwar chuckles.

"You were a boy always searching."

Dando's eyes soften,
finding joy in good memories.

SEEING THE SAME SUN

My rake's fingers scrape dirt,
giving off the sound of hard work.

Old Anwar says,
"There is something else Amira gets from you—
farm sense."

Dando agrees.
"That child is good with sheep and wheat.
I believe she could
have a gift for learning letters."

I can't even pretend to work now.
My ears are eager to do their job.

I rock my rake's handle,
but it's hardly moving.

"Teach Amira to read," Old Anwar says.

My raking has stopped.
I do not want to miss a word.

My cow plop pile has begun to call flies
to its rising fumes.
They're happy to play among the moist,
lingering mounds.

Dando sets his hands
at Old Anwar's back,
gives a playful tug.

"Old Anwar,
you and I see the same sun on the horizon.
It would bring me such pleasure
to teach Amira to read,
but I cannot convince my wife of this."

Old Anwar places *his* hand
at my father's waist,
echoing the gesture.

He says,
"Your girl's glint should be allowed to
shine even brighter."

My father nods,
agreeing.

Old Anwar and Dando,
seeing the same sun.

BROKEN-BOTTLE DOLLY

Leila has found a cracked plastic bottle,
an abandoned shell.

The bottle's clear body is packed with dirt,
thick with *goz*,
filled with brown,
right up to its neck.

A swatch of green makes this baby doll's dress.

Leila loves her, even with no head.
Even with no arms or legs.
Even with the tiny, jagged crack at her bottom,
leaking grains of *goz*.

Soon that dirt-filled dolly has a name.

Leila proclaims her toy's birth.
Smiles at the sight.

She invents silly wispy voices
that bring her baby to life.

"Sweet little Salma."

Leila murmurs and sighs at the newborn
nestled in her stumpy arms.

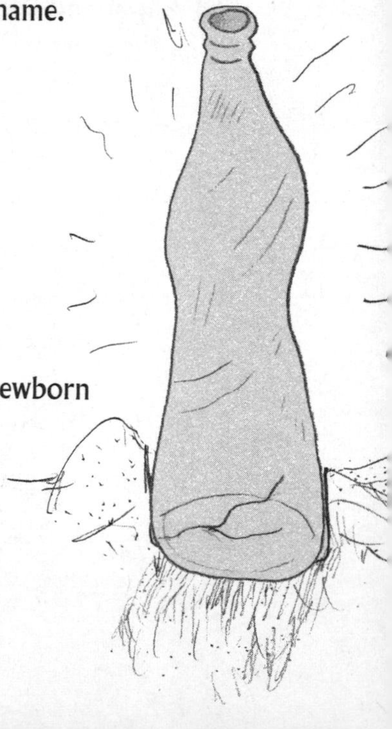

TOY BATTLES

"I found it first!" shouts Gamal.
Leila squeals, "No, mine!"
Gamal and Leila each yank
to claim the cracked,
plastic,
left-for-dead bottle.

Leila cries, "*My* child, *my* baby."
"Mine!" claims Gamal.

He pulls loose the green sheath dress.
Snatches the bottle from Leila's hungry hands,
runs off fast.

Gamal won't look behind him, at us.
He settles on a patch of sand
far enough from Leila so that she can't chase him
on her turned-in feet.

He's escaped,
but is close enough to taunt Leila.

Vrrraahhoooom comes from someplace deep
in this greedy boy
as he rams baby Salma on her side.

Vrrraaaahhoooms that broken bottle
back and forth on the sand.

He sneers.
"This is no baby doll! It's my jeep!"

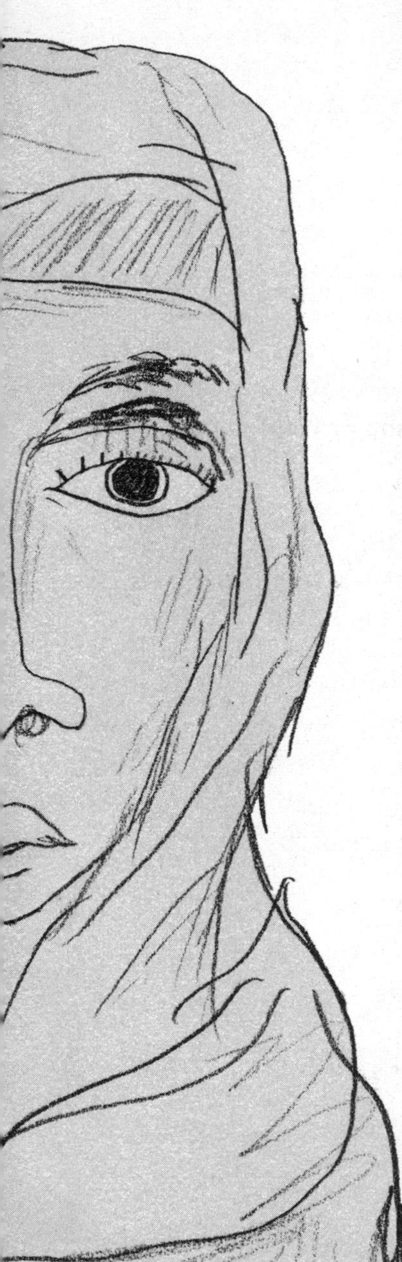

EYES

Ever since Dando told me
of war,
and Muma, of the Janjaweed,

I've noticed
a strange shadow
in people's eyes.

This dim, shapeless thing
has been lurking.

This shaded expression
that has no name
has settled itself
in glances and unspoken foreboding.

I look closer,
trying to know
what is in
the eyes of my village neighbors,
and of Dando and Muma.

It's something
other
than concern about the hiding moon.

In time, I see.

Eyes tell
what is inside.

Muma and Dando,
they speak,
they work,
they move about each day
with their regular
here-and-there.

But their eyes say
something is *not* regular.

Their eyes confess fright,
as if every breeze,
every shadow,
every leaf
whispers a warning.

I look and look
so deep
into
the odd,
scared,
uneasy
that has settled in so many eyes.

When I dare to cut a stare,
then hold the gaze
of a grown-up,
my own eyes ask,

Why?

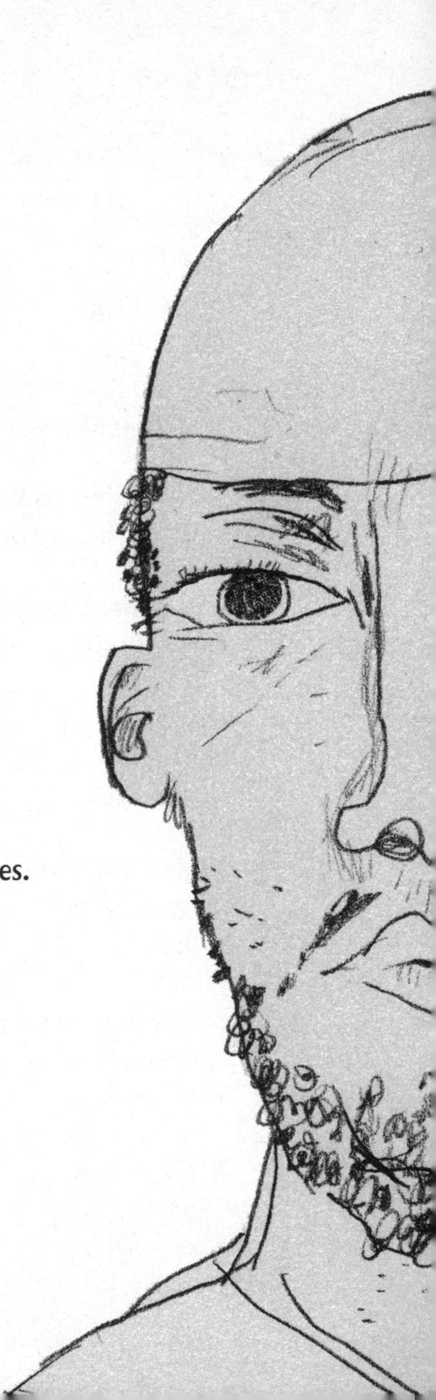

DOTS

Twig, you are lazy today.
All you do is poke.

Dot.
Dot.

Tiny messes on the sand's surface.

Dot.
Dot.

Dot...dot...dot...

There is so much wind today.
That is good.

It can sweep away these nothing-dots.
Good-bye, lazy twig-pokes!

Lots of dots
blow down
to just a few.

But, *aakh*—then I see
the possibilities
in dots.

Wait, wind! Please stop!
You are lifting away
what could have been:

Bird footprints.
A spray of stars.

Eyes peeking out from a wall of goz.
Split beans, spilled.

So many wonders arise from

Dot.
Dot.
Dot.

I wish I'd seen them sooner.

WAKING, WALKING, WATER

We rise
before the sun
pierces the night.

Before dawn has a chance
to press
on our heads,
baking us
with unrelenting heat.

Muma rouses me,
sounding as crisp as wind.
"Amira, come."

Does my mother ever sleep?

We wake
to walk,
many miles there,
many back.

Taking so long, this journey.

Slowly
we go
for water.

Our plastic jugs are empty on our way
to the river's gate.

But, *aakh*, the return.
Aakh, the ache
in our backs,
through our legs.

The riverbed fills our empty, wanting vessels
with the wet,
sloshing promise of water.

Weighing heavily,
pulling our pails
down,
down,
down,
bending branches into arcs
that make
the ache
stay
all day.

FAMILY PICTURES

Muma:

strong face,
beautiful,
square.

Her *toob*
a column of twig-strokes
I strike in the sand:
sweesh-swoosh!
sweesh-swoosh!

Spilling from all sides
of her stands-so-proud body,
covering every part of my mother.

Except for her wide, loving eyes.
Except for her wide-fingered hands.
Except for her wide, flat feet.

Two stretched shapes
peeking out from the twig-strokes that make
sweesh-swoosh.

Dando:

body,
a box.

Face,
so oval.

Stubbled chin,
a triangle
decorated,

dot…dot…
dot…

to show hair
trying to grow.

Dando's eyes,
wells of wisdom.

Dando,
who sees what is possible in me.

I craft his wise eyes by digging
two more dot-dots,
deep.

Leila:

all of her bowed.
Legs,
arms,
neck,

ears.

Arcs,
curves,
half circles
reaching
to become
straight lines.

Leila's face:
open,
ready,
steady gaze,
dimple-cheeks,
framed by a billowing *tarha*.

Me:

Amira Bright.

Eyes like my father's.
Deep wells
seeking
hope on the horizon.

Seeing the sun's
open hand,
distant.

ETERNITY

Muma's wedding *toob*,
tightly folded,
tucked safely away.

My mother shows me the cotton sheath's threading.

A hibiscus flower,
stitched in its corner.

A special wedding gift
from her own mother's hand.
My grandmother,
passed on,
now a memory.

Muma lets me touch the *toob*'s delicate embroidery.
These stitches are a joy-swirl.

One of the lovely things
about Muma's long-held traditions.

"Beauty," I say.

"Try it on, Amira."

Muma's calloused hands
drape the sheer fabric around my face.

Softly she says,
"Yours someday."

MELON BELLY

I sprinkle millet in Nali's pen.
Today she's more hungry than usual.

She chomps fast,
as if tomorrow will never come.

Muma asks, "Do you see Nali's gait, so lopsided?
And her belly, so plump?"

"Too much millet," I say.
"She's becoming greedy."

Muma calls Nali.
She bumbles slowly, waddling.
Muma puts her hand on the roundest part
of Nali's middle.

"Feel," she instructs,
guiding my hand to the same wide spot
on my sheep's body.

At the place where my palm presses tight,
it's as if Nali has swallowed a melon,
never having chewed it.

"Nali!" I scold.
"Soon your legs will not be able to hold you."

I start to draw my hand away,
but Muma will not let me.
"Keep it there, Amira.
Wait for a moment.
Close your eyes to feel what has come to Nali."

This is silly.
I don't want to do it,
but I follow Muma's directions.

"All I feel is a too-full tummy."

Muma hushes me.
"Quiet now," she says.
"Let Nali relax.
Her ears are pressed down. She's tense."

I open my eyes to see.
Muma is right. Nali's pink-tipped ears are wilted.
"Rub the spot. That will help," Muma suggests.

"Help what?" I want to know.

Before Muma answers,
something from inside my sheep jerks,
then presses back at my hand,
telling me what's inside Nali.

I have felt melon bellies on our animals before,
so I know.

"Nali, you will soon birth a baby lamb!"

Muma's expression
fills with as much expectation as Nali's tummy.

She rests her hand next to mine.
Together we rub-rub Nali's belly,
ripe with new life.

THE HABOOB

I hear its thunder before I see its face.
The sky is the color of a glistening onion,
bulging brown at its edges.

It brings a serpent of wind
with a yellow tail
trailing all the way to the horizon.

The *haboob* crackles a warning
as it spins from far off,
then closer.

I can smell its moisture
swelling in the clouds.

When I first see the *haboob* coming,
I'm taken with its twisting beauty.

I know these sandstorms are dangerous,
but they are a giant wonder.

"Look, Dando! The sky is spinning a rope!"

DEMON!

Dando does not speak.
Not to me.
Not to anyone.

He's scurrying like a busy cricket,
rushing
to cover
our home's open places
with sheets of tin,
clamped tight.

Muma is inside our house,
just as busy,
laying tarps
over washbasins,
and our sleeping pallets.

The other villagers are as frenzied as Dando,
moving quickly,
so frightened.

Their worried shouts punch at the afternoon.
Some are shrieking.

I race to our livestock pen to find Nali.
But she is nowhere.
"Nali!" I call.

I hear a neighbor's plea. "*Haboob,* be merciful!"

Our goats and chickens
send their own prayers into the wind,
bleating,
squawking.

I flap my arms in front of me,
like so many hurried hens,
shoo-shooing our animals
under their tin-covered
shelters.

Soon all the other villagers have escaped
to their homes.

Dando and I are the only ones outside.

Finally, Dando calls to me,
"Amira, we must get with your mother
so that I can cover the door! Hurry, child!"

The land is now spraying its dust,
flinging gritty bits
of *goz*.

The *haboob*'s wide-open mouth
collects the sand,
then spits it in all directions.

As the storm hurls forward,
I watch the grasses go flat
under its weight.

Dando's voice
is shrouded
by the *haboob*'s stomp-noise.

"This dust storm has the lash of a demon!"

WORRY

Dando's gaze is stern.
He yanks at me to follow him home.

I rear back, refusing.
"No, Dando! I must find Nali."

Sand rips at our clothing,
at our skin.

Stings the insides of my nose and ears.

My father's hair
is doused in a powdery brown cap.
So much flying *goz*.

I hold tightly to Dando's leg,
forcing him to let me stay outside.

"Dando, please. I need to look for Nali!"

"There is no time for that, Amira," Dando insists.

Muma calls
from the one uncovered opening in our house.

"This *haboob*,
she is roaring forward!"

"Amira is being obstinate,"
Dando calls back.

Muma is trying to tell us something,
but the wind's moan has muffled her.

Dando shields his face
with the crook of one arm.

Works hard
to scoop me off the sand
with his free hand.

I can't come.
I won't leave my sheep
to be swallowed up in this
monster's wake.

Through squinted eyes,
I watch the *haboob* dance.

"Nali!"

DUST WALL

I don't know
what the rippling curtain of yellow,
corded in black,
will do next,
but I'm afraid it has taken Nali in its grip.

This storm swirls
like the fabric of a wind-whipped *toob*.

The wall of dust
made by its growing rope
is now so thick,
I can barely see.

I'm wincing,
praying to find my sheep.

Dando has become very angry.
"Amira!"

He tries to pull me toward our house
by dragging his leg.

This won't work.
We're sheaths of wheat
against the *haboob*'s weight.

I beg Dando, "Let. Me. Stay. To find—Na—!"
The wind yowls.

In just moments,
the *haboob* will be up close.

I bury my face
at the tops of Dando's feet.

Then,
as if the *haboob* has come to a quick decision,
she swerves upward.

Gathers her flailing wind.
Hurls away in a sharp slant,
a proud bird showing off her tail.

I blink,
brush at the crusty film
now covering all of me.

I'm coughing.
Hard, hard coughing.

BLEAT—RELIEF!

The *haboob* is gone.
The storm has left soft dune blankets.

It has flattened our crops.
It has coated our chickens
in *goz* dust.

It has dressed our goats
and cows
in sand-matted fur.

Everything grows still.

Leila wails from inside our house.

My coughing turns to spitting dust.
I hear a long bleat.
Pained, but strong.

I know that rounded *bahhh...bahhh...*

Muma calls,
"Amira, I tried to tell you, but the *haboob*'s
noise had grown too loud.
Nali is here. I'd managed to get her inside."

In one long breath,
I release
relief.

My sheep and her unborn baby—safe.

AFTERWARD

We spend the rest of our day
and evening
cleaning sand
from the tarps
and anything they failed to cover.

This is gritty work.
The *haboob*'s powder rests inside,
between,
under,
and on everything.

Dando is silent while we work.
Muma, too.
Leila naps, but wakes often,
startled.

As night falls,
Muma encourages me to settle on my pallet.
She has allowed Nali to sleep beside me.

My own sleep won't come.
Nali's breathing is a soft comfort,
yet I'm still enthralled
by the *haboob*'s howling whirl.

The memory of its twisting beauty
is a dream-swirl in my mind.

DANDO'S CONFESSION

Muma rocks Leila, who, like me,
can't sleep.
She's fitful, cranky.

I'm the opposite.
I'm filled with the excitement that lingers
after fast dancing.

Dando tries to calm me,
rubbing slow circles in my back.
"You frightened me today," he says quietly.

"Dando, you are never afraid."

"I was this afternoon, Amira.
I thought I might lose you."

"But Dando,
I thought I'd lost Nali."

"I understand about Nali, but you disobeyed me.
The *haboob* destroys. It is not a game."

"Dando—"

"Enough, Amira!"

I dare not speak after Dando.

I find my own quiet
by listening to our village birds
settling after the storm.

I pet Nali's ears,
rest my hands on her melon belly.

As sleep's veil spreads over me,
Dando asks,
"Where do you get such self-determination?"

I whisper softly
so that my father can't hear when I ask,
"Where do you?"

LIZARD

The *haboob*'s flying dust
had blinded me.

Leila's ditty tells me this:

"My sister is a lizard.

Silly, slippery.
Slippery, silly.

Dancing in the windstorm.
Dancing in the windstorm.

Playing.
Prancing.

Playing.
Prancing.

Swirling at her own party
with a haboob *monster,*
while Muma and Dando
scurry
and worry
for my
silly,
slippery
swirling
sister.

Dancing.
Playing.
Prancing.

In scary monster winds,
my silly,
slippery
lizard sister
only cares about
her own tail."

To Leila, this ditty is fun to sing.
But it doesn't make me smile.

It shows me I've been selfish.

APOLOGY

I race to find Dando
in the far-off fields.

He is silently tending his flattened tomato plants,
buried in deep thoughts,
frowning,
wrapped in concentration.

My shadow startles him.
"Amira—"

I allow Dando a moment.
But my words don't want to wait.

I *talk* and *talk*.
And blurt.
And let it all tumble
out of me.

Like the *haboob*'s wild wind,
my *talking, talking*
flies every which way.

I recount the storm
as if it's happening this
very minute.

My ears and neck
grow warm in the retelling.

I'm *talking, talking.*
Fast, fast *talking.*
I want to say so much.

Dando gently places his palm
at the top of my head.

"Daughter, what is it you are trying to tell me?"

I finally land on the words I'm meaning to say:

"I'm sorry."

Dando scoops me into a hug,
arms tender, and strong, too.

Loving loaves,
holding tight,
he whispers sweetly,
close at my ear.

Kisses his obstinate girl.
"Oh, Amira Bright."

NALI'S GIFT

Nali has settled herself
on a patch of dried grasses
at the far end
of our livestock pen.

She rests on her side,
panting, bleating,
eyes half-closed
to slits.

Above,
the sky has prepared for
something special by
decorating this night with
star-spray.

Speckled bits of silver
against a blue-black cap.

"It will be soon," Muma says,
and I know just what she means.

"Can I stay here with Nali?" I ask.

Muma cups my cheeks.
"Let her be."

We return to our house.
I try to sleep,
but don't.

As soon as the tiniest finger
of morning's light peels back the night,
I race to the pen.

Nali is up on all her legs.
So is her new lamb!

The scrawny creature
is a white-coated
baby
with sharp limbs,
tilted ears,
dark eyes
pooled with wonderings.

Nali looks pleased to see me.
The lamb's frail legs buckle,
then fold.

She lands, belly flat, limbs splayed,
on the matted grasses beneath.

Nali nuzzles her child,
coaxes the lamb.

Gets this newborn back to standing,
then to suckling underneath her.

I call from the pen,
"Muma, Dando, Leila,
come see!"

FLITTER

Leila is first,
both her small brown hands
smoothing the baby's thin fur,
pet-petting
from the lamb's ears
to her flittering tail.

Leila asks, "What will we call her?"

I needn't think too hard.
The name just comes.

"Flitter," I say.

SAND SHEEP

Drawing sheep
in the sand
with my twig
is easy.

Nali:
circle body,
curls for fur,
legs short.

Eyes, nostrils,
dot-dot,
dot-dot.

Flitter:
rectangle middle,
triangle ears.

Legs,
eight strokes
to outline four spindly limbs.

Tail,
a scribbly blur,
to show how that happy
back-end nub
never stops
swatting flies.

PEEK-AND-PRANCE

Silly Flitter waits for me
each morning
when I arrive at her pen.

She hides to the side
of Nali's still-plump belly,
thinking I can't see
her bony shins or nubby tail,
flicking fast from her rump.

I go along with this game
of hide-and-find,
calling her name
until she peeks,
then prances
to show me,
Here I am!

DAWN

We start the day
with a meal of our farm's best fruit.

Mangoes,
spilling
their tangy insides
when Leila and I
bury our noses and teeth
to slurp at their pillowy middles.

Ya—it is a good morning.

After we eat, Dando and Old Anwar
go to the far fields.
Their bodies paint blue silhouettes
against dawn's tawny drape.

SUDDEN GUST

For Muma and me,
this is our day to roll dough
into loaves
that will settle in the shade
of our farm's leafiest tree,
before baking in covered clay.

Muma shows me the right way
for pressing the heel of my hand
to flatten the supple mounds.

"Do it with your whole soul,"
she instructs. "Bread is best
when prepared from a woman's
deepest self."

Muma has given Leila a clump of dough.
My sister hums, pats, plays with her soft ball.

Morning's birds glide on the horizon.
Muma joins Leila's humming.
Me, too.
I like this time together.

In a quick gust, the wind picks up,
then thrusts forward.

Another *haboob*?
So soon?

HAMMERING

Something thunders.
I hear hammering
from a place above.

Muma's face is pinched.
My mother's expression flashes
with the dark
fright
I'd seen lurking
in many eyes from my village.

Muma hushes me,
moves slowly
from our home's central room
to outside.

Fierce pounding, so strong,
brings more than just wind.
It's as if our village has been plunged
inside a hollow gourd
that is being shaken by violent hands.

The hammering bangs loud now.
Earsplitting sound!

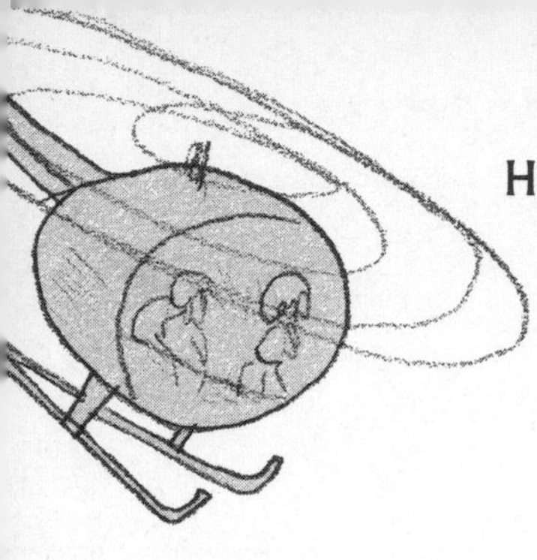

HAPPENING?

Muma flips our sleeping pallets
up from their resting place on the floor.
She wraps one around Leila, then me.

Tucks us in a corner.
"Stay put!" she orders,
then races toward the crop fields.

Leila obeys,
pulls her knees beneath her,
tucks her head on the floor.
Hides her whole self under
the mat's slats.

I follow after Muma,
but soon wish I'd done as I was told.

Suddenly, I see.
This is no *haboob.*
It's the Janjaweed!

All place and time,
mind and breath
become blurred chaos,
shuddering frantically.

Is?
This?
Truly?
Happening?

Helicopters
chopping
the clouds.
Shrieking people.
Men on horseback.
Jallabiyas flailing.
Camels with mashed-in noses.
Galloping fast in a heated race.
Coming closer.

Wicked riders advancing.

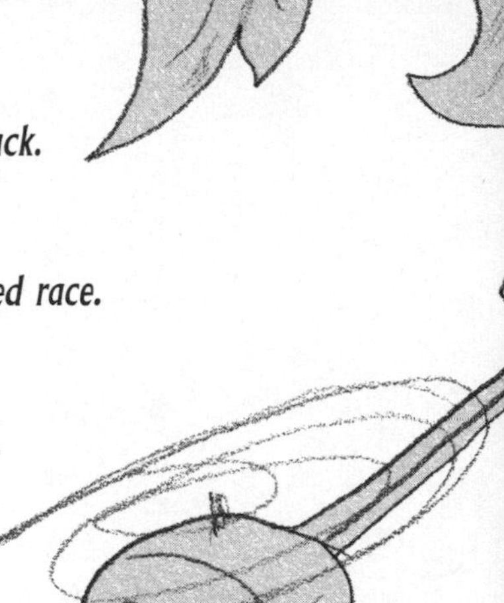

Can?
This?
Really?
Be?
Happening?

Men with eyes
the color of rotted squash.
Preparing to slaughter.

How?
Is?
This?
Happening?

Hooves.
Hard pounding.

Bullets
spraying
into crowds.

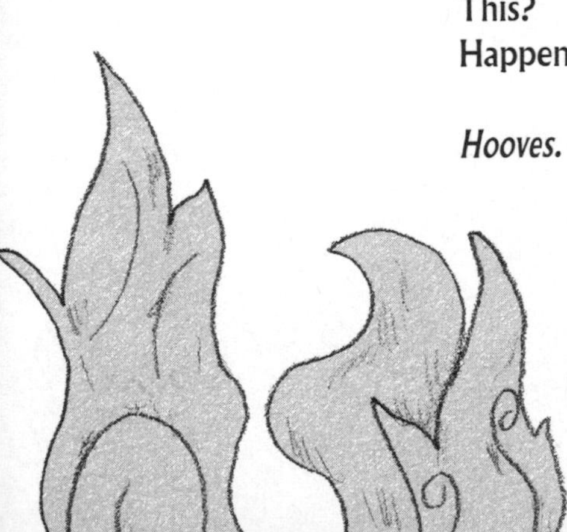

Screams.
So many screams.

Is that Muma up ahead?
Frantic?
Running?

Is that Dando—falling?
Snapped to the grass,
blood spurting from his back?

Is that my own voice,
calling, "Noooo!"?
Then come torches.
Flames hurled to the roofs.
Our livestock pen alight with fire.
Nali?
Is that Nali?

The fires have snatched her up
in their wild jaws.

Another scream that sounds like me.
Pleading,
"Noooo!"

Those fires have hungry tongues.

They swallow Nali whole.

Happening?
Happening?
Happening?

My sheep ignites
into a fluffy pillow of flames,
bleating for mercy.

"Noooo!"

Goz dust has clouded all sight.

Then, as suddenly as it came,
the hammering recedes.

Gallops cease.

Smoke rises,
its weighty blackness stinging
the insides of my nose.

It is the tortured sounds
of gagging
that tell me
I am still alive.

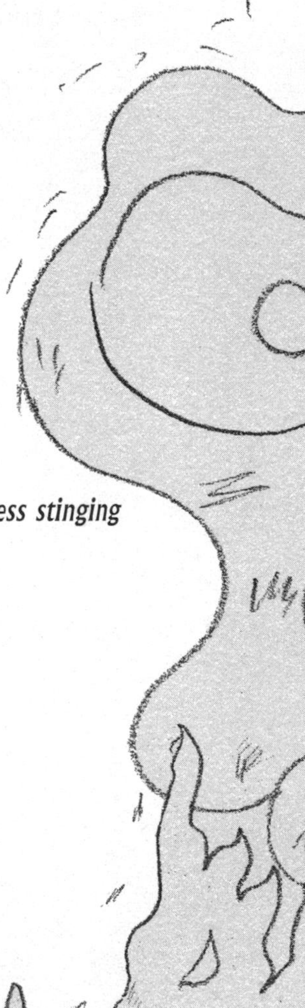

SHOCK

Quick-crack.
        Brittle twig—snapped.

Nali—dead!
Dando—dead!

        My whole heart.

        A sudden break.

        My Bright,
        turned black.
                Stricken!

TOGETHER

Muma
moves quickly,
rolling mats,
gathering fabric
and food.

Old Anwar
helps Muma
collect what she can.

He's brought his donkey
to our house.
With him, too,
is Gamal
whose face is singed
at the place
where his ear meets his neck.

His burns are the crisscross
of a spider's web.

Open skin.
Raw.

Gamal, an orphan now.

Old Anwar peels the curled-open skin
from Gamal's neck.

Patches his burns
with a root poultice.

Gamal winces,
whimpers,
bites hard on his lip.

Leila hangs tight
to Muma's *toob.*

Old Anwar says,
"We must stay together."

CALLING

"Flitter!"
I expect her to come,
my obedient lamb,
Nali's child.

"Flitter!"
I call and call.

But all I hear
is the wind, gasping.

Even the air around us
is struggling to find its balance.

The sound of my *toob*'s fabric
flapping around my face
is an annoyance.

I call and call.
But still no Flitter.

What else is possible? my
worries ask.

It could be that Flitter is
playing
a new hiding game of *Here I
am*.

Yes, that's it. That's what it could be.

Silly lamb!
Funny Flitter.

But by nightfall,
even when I call,
Flitter does not come running.

NOWHERE

Next day.
No Flitter still.

I call when I wake.
I call when the afternoon sun
is a high, hot ball.

At dusk, I call.

I crawl under,
behind,
and into charred bushes,
looking for Flitter,
who is not there.

I comb the grain shed's corners,
now ransacked and smelling of
burned wood.

"Flitter! Flitter!"

My sheep's baby lamb
is nowhere.

Muma holds me,
tenderly, quietly.

Touches her forehead to mine,
whispers,
"Flitter is gone."

FLEEING

Tonight. Black. Silent.
Thick. Hot. Dry.

The darkest night
our village will ever see.

Muma is firm.
"Only take what you can carry."

I choose my twig.

Leila wants her broken-bottle dolly,
but its plastic is melted and mashed.

She's managed to find her baby's
green cotton swatch, which she holds firm
in her little fist
while sucking on her hand for comfort,
like when *she* was a baby.

Muma's only bundle is Leila,
who she's tied to her back.

Each of us bears the heaviest weight of all,
anguish, unmovable,
like so many mud-brick sacks.

ASHES

With us are villagers
I don't fully know.

Mostly women,
some men,
boys,
girls,
babies.

Our animals didn't survive.
Old Anwar's donkey
carries food rations,
and what little else we've brought.

We walk,
forming a crooked,
curving line.

We snake,
single file,
stitches along the desert's hem.

One silent step at a time,
we wind our way
to who-knows-where.

"Where are we going?" I ask.
"To safety," Muma says.

Her clipped, quiet words tell me
I'm to ask no more questions.

No time for even a backward glance.
But I can't help it.
I look behind me.

Our home has been burned
to blackened bits
of thatch,
laced with memories
of what once had been:

Golden wheat.
Milking goats.
Okra.

The last remnant I see
is Muma's wedding *toob,*
now a little hill of ash,
resting atop a pile of soot,
its fringed edge
flicking in the breeze,
waving good-bye.

SOLES

Old Anwar explains:
"Our direction depends on the safest path,
where harmless land leads us.
We can only know the way as it reveals itself.
Our journey's end will be shown as we go."

We walk on dogged feet
for nights
and nights
and nights.

We can go only when it's dark.
When we can't be seen.
When there is no Janjaweed.

It's not safe during the day.

Miles and miles in nighttime.
My soles are melting.
I'm so thirsty.
We must ration the little bit of water we have.

I try not to whine,
but I do.

Muma says,
"Don't think of water.
It will make you crave it more."

Leila is the fortunate one.
Muma says we can move faster
if she carries Leila.

My dwarfed sister
starts out riding and resting
on Muma's back.

If only I were small enough to ride
on my mother's hunched body.
I could press my chest right to her.
I could send my heart's drumming to Muma's heart,
sliced with sorrow.

Gamal keeps touching
at the place
on his neck
that has crusted pus
collecting at its edges.

He's also trying hard not to whine.

FORWARD

Next night.

We take comfort
in the coolness of trees
whose leaves
have shaded the ground
beneath our feet.

But we must not linger.

The luxury of an easy walk
is something we can't afford.
We forge forward.
Yesterday is a land gone.

"Keep moving," says Old Anwar.

There's nothing old or slow about this man,
my father's rival-friend,
who has buried his silly tomato contest
with the memory of Dando's last breath.

FOOTPRINTS

I pretend
Dando is walking alongside me,
holding my hand,
helping me through this.

I pretend
to see his footprints,
long,
shaped like flattened leaves,
marking the sand,
setting down a path
for my own small
feet
to follow.

I pretend
Dando is here,
stepping heavily,
heel-toe,
heel-toe,
leading me,
lovingly.

I pretend
so, so hard,
with my whole
heart.

But it's fruitless.

This so-hard pretending
doesn't work.

My father's footprints,
nowhere.

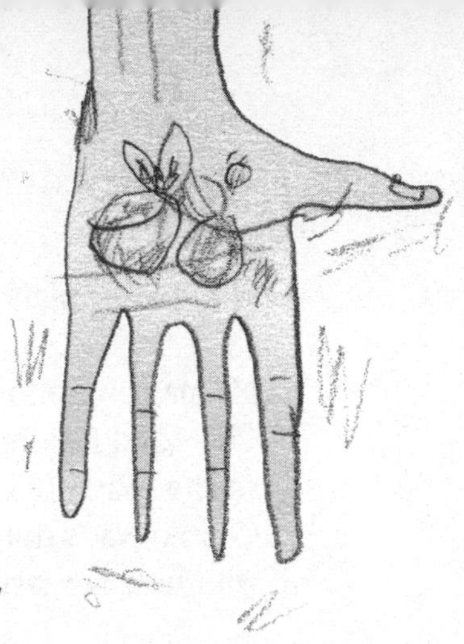

HUNGRY

Our weary feet
keep moving
silently
across vast sheets of sand,
spreading wide
for miles,
rolled out like a rippling carpet,
leading to uncertainty.

I'm allowed only one meal from Old Anwar's pouch:

A palmful of peanuts.
A rodent's bit of rice.
A clump of corn,
swallowed down with the little bit of wet
I can summon from my tongue.

Gamal and the other children
have all been rationed the same.

Greedy Gamal doesn't nibble.
He mashes his ration into one bite,
devours the morsels that must sustain him
until tomorrow.

"Chew slow," I warn. "Make it last."
Gamal cries, "I can't."

STUBBORN

Night after night.

Muma can no longer carry Leila.
Our food rations have dwindled,
so she insists that my sister ride atop
Old Anwar's donkey,
who now has less to carry.

Leila refuses.
"I can walk," she squeals.
"Do not argue," Muma says. "Not now."
"I. Can. Walk!"
Leila will not budge.

She has pinned her bottom to the ground,
arms laced around herself,
unmoving,
and churning up too much noise.

"I. Can. Walk!"

Muma has reached the end of her tether.
She is frustrated.
Leila is making it worse.

"I. Can. Walk!"

Muma tries to reason with Leila.

"You *can* walk.
We know you are able.
But now you must ride."

"No donkey!"
Like such a baby, Leila cries.

Muma clasps both Leila's shoulders,
preparing to scold
my stubborn sister.

Old Anwar intervenes,
clasping, too,
Muma's forearms.

He is stern when he says,
"Let the child walk."

NO MOON

As we make our way,
we stay quiet,
and always hidden.
It's not safe.

If *Sayidda* Moon decides to flee, too,
if, like us, she wants to hide,
this time we do not call her.

This time only,
we let *Sayidda* Moon conceal her face.

Old Anwar tells us
we're now in a region where
militia comb,
looking for ways to scrub the territory
clean
of anyone they deem
a threat.

"This war," he says. "It is a fight over land and rights.
Such a wicked conflict.
Africans and Arabs, each feeling entitled.
Greed and arrogance have brought bloodshed."

Best to let *Sayidda* Moon's light rest
behind cloud cover.

These nights,
never ending.

CURSED

I've lost my twig!

I beg Muma,
"We must turn back!"

I know this can't happen,
but I can think of
no other way.

Muma tries to comfort me.
"You will find another."

This doesn't help.
There *is* no other
turning-twelve twig.

There *is* no other gift from Dando.

Our village superstition is true.

The hidden moon
has brought
bad
luck!

MISERY

Old Anwar's donkey
forces breaths
through loose,
thirsty lips.

We keep walking.
In darkness.
Not talking.
Only wanting
this misery over.

QUEASY

How long,
and how many
nights have we walked,
single file?

And since we still don't know where.

And since
my whole body aches.

And since
my stomach churns
with hunger,
I can't tell how much longer.

DAZED

All sense,
gone.

I know only to pray
to Allah:

Make this end soon.

QUICK-STREAM

There's only one way to get relief.

Squat behind a bush.
Hike my *toob* fabric.
Let go fast.
Release a stream.
          Hurry!
          Hurry!
I must rush
to keep up
with the group.

It's a miracle there's any water
anywhere on my parched
insides.

Perhaps I'm part camel,
storing up
for this
long walk
on a path of despair.

DISPLACED

I don't know what day this is,
but I do know it *is* day.

First light brings a promise.
Up ahead, we see it.

Old Anwar tells us,
"We are at Kalma."

The sign says:
DISPLACED PEOPLE'S CAMP.

Kalma's outsides are dressed
in wire necklaces,
and fences,
and tents
where workers welcome us
by shoving our tired,
dirty,
very thirsty,
dusty bodies
through slices of fabric
that open onto shanties
crammed together,
like peanuts in a too-tight shell.

Everywhere I look,
I see
people, people, and more people.

I'm glad to stop walking.
I'm glad we have finally reached who-knows-where.
But already I do not like this place.

PART 2

KALMA

April 2004–June 2004

SCRAPS

Our house is made of rice-bag scraps.

No walls,
only plastic flaps,
billowing
in stale breezes.

The roof of this rice-bag house
is patched together
from the roots
of diseased, brittle trees.

This place,
this dwelling,
a misshapen dome.

Home?

DISBELIEF

Dando,
in this new land,
memories haunt me.

In my mind's shadow,
that ugly day
will not go away.

Dando,
I watched you fall,
but I can't
believe
what I saw.

I remember the bullets,
hammering.

I remember screams,
and shrieks,
and prayers for mercy.

But
it doesn't
seem true.

It's worse than a horror-dream.

Bodies
dropping
like overripe mangoes,
surrendered
from their places on a beautiful tree.

But what fell
—*thud!*—
to the sand
was not sweet fruit.

One—*thud!*—then another,
then one more,
until many men
and women
and boys and girls
littered our land.

What fell
was anyone
who tried to flee
on that violent day
when bullets flung
from no place I know.

When those gunshots
flew with no warning,
or expectation,
or good reason
to leave fathers,

brothers,
daughters,
elders—and my Dando—
dead
on the blood-smeared sand.

I can't believe
what I saw.

How can this be?

Dando,
we are in a strange place,
without you.

Are you really gone?

I just can't believe it.

VANISHING

Something
is
s l i p p i n g
a w a y.

Draining
out
from
deep
in
me.

G r a i n s
o f
g
o
z

a l l
f
a
l
l
i n g...

I...I...t-r-r-r-y to call after them,
as I would
a running-off lamb.

"Come heeere...come...heeere...."

I work to bring words,
but...but...
get only half sound.

Slurred murmur.

Broken whisper
s l i d i n g
off.

Me,
struggling to speak.

Stammering.

"Come
heeere....
Come..."

My voice
v a n i s h i n g.

MOURNING

Muma weeps quietly.
She waits
for night to fall,
so we won't witness
her crying.

She waits
for the deepest part of the dark,
thinking she can hide
from Leila,
from me.

My sister is restless, but sleeping.
I'm fully awake,
blinking
into night's nothingness.

The sky is clear.
It offers blue light,
illuminates the inside of our shack.

Lets me see
my mother's body
pulled into a knot.

When the worst of it overtakes Muma,
she stifles sobs,
only half-released by
the trembling widow
she's become.

Muma doesn't want us to watch her
wipe hard at her eyes
with the backs
of both hands.

Muma, so proud,
doesn't want us to know
she's given way to grief's
weakness.

My proud mother thinks
she's hiding.

But when morning comes,
she wakes with a tear-stained face.

RUBBER TWIGS

The soil at Kalma is dark,
dry,
smelly.

Oh, that odor!
Worse than cow plop.

Thick and sickening, it is.

A sour mix of rot
and sorrow,
rancid trash,
decaying memories.

Kalma's twigs
are limp,
rubbery
reeds of nothing.

It's as if they've lost all will
to grow.

These sickly sticks don't spread
or poke—they wither.

I try to snap a twig from trees
and bushes,
but to do it, I must wrestle.

I must twist and twist,
with gritted teeth,
fighting to break off a branch,
while at the same time working
to breathe away
the filthy earth,
stinking,
and rising to greet me.

There is so much sadness
in Kalma's dirt.

No life in this camp's branches.

Flimsy,
wiry,
withering souls
whose trees are just as weak.

I don't want to draw,
at all,
on this rancid land,
with these meek,
rubber strands,
so bendy.

My hand's dance is gone.
My *sparrow* has lost its wings.

Goz, I miss you.

SILENCE

What started
        as slipping,
what began as a vanishing voice,
        is now fully gone.

        I

can

        not

speak.

Words,
like tugged teeth.

Yanked
from every part of me.

CROWDED KALMA

Everywhere bodies:
all of us sweaty,
desperate,
uprooted.

Everywhere bodies:
ride rickety bikes,
held together
with rust
and spit
and trust.

Everywhere bodies:
clustered and wondering,
Why are we here?

Everywhere bodies:
We are tribespeople,
farmers,
villagers.

Huddled
at wide-open trash bins.

Poking down in
with the rubber twigs,
fishing for food,
no matter how foul.

Everywhere bodies:
We've fled
peaceful homes.

Beautiful villages.
Abundant farms.

Forced to leave
prosperous lands
whose unfortunate luck
has set us in unsafe places,
making us prey
to the Janjaweed.

Everywhere bodies:
now packed together
in crowded Kalma.

Everywhere bodies:
mix-and-match
cultures,
clashing,
smashing
against
one another.

All so different,
but also the same.

Everywhere bodies:
with one common trait.

Sad eyes
turned downward,
searching for answers
not found in smelly dirt.

ECHO

Chirpity
chirpity
chwreeeep
chwreeeeeeeeep...
Chwrrrreep...

I hear a bird,
distant,
low-calling
from some smothered place
that feels like it belongs to me.

Where is *that sound coming from?*

The springs in my mind?
The way back of my tongue?
From behind my belly button?

Where is *that chirpity bird?*

Who's holding that chwreeep-chwreeeeep...?

One thing I know for certain.
The chirpity bird is fighting to make sound.

It's tamped down,
pressed back,
suffocated.

Wanting,
so much wanting
to *chwreeeep*
free.

This strangled birdsong
can't escape its own echo.

LOCKED

Muma tries,
but it's useless.

She coaxes,
coddles,
as if feeding a finicky child.

"Start slow," she says.
"A bit at a time.
Just a little."

She's working to soften
her twisted brows,
hoping this will somehow help.

"One word, Amira.
You can do it, child.
A whisper to begin.
Can you say
Muma?
Leila?"

She speaks to me
as if I've forgotten her name,
and Leila's.

I *know* the names,
but can't *say* them.

I shake my head.

Pain-clouds rise in Muma's eyes.
She takes both my hands in hers.
Holds them.
Kneads them,
as if she's shaping dough.

"Amira, sorrow's fence
has locked you in," she says.
"The only way out
is through time."

THE WATER GIVER

There is water at Kalma.
But it doesn't collect or flow
from the river's mouth.

Here,
water is doled out,
in what feel like pinched droplets.

All day we wait
in lines of longing.

Waiting on wet
from the water giver's hand.

The water giver,
a man
strictly sticking to his rules of ration:
    one gallon
    per person
    per day

It's the women who stand
in the lines of longing,
waiting on wet from the water giver's hand:

    one plastic jug
    for washing
    cleaning
    bathing
    drinking

The water giver's hand must fill many needs.

Today,
while Muma and I stand
and wait,
I pray the water giver's one-gallon grip
will slip,
and somehow
let more wet spill into our jug.

It's hard
waiting for what is not enough.

It hurts
to pray for deprivation.

It's like wishing on a thimble.

THE FLICKER BOX

Kalma is home to a big flicker box.
On our farm there was no such thing.

A flicker box—
lighted,
loud,
blaring sound.

A flicker box—
nailed high up
on an iron pole
so that everyone can see
what flickers out
from its shiny square face.

Flickering,
flickering.

Pink people.
Laughing herky-jerky

Flickering,
flickering.

Noisy colors I've never seen.
Shapes that whirl.

Teethy mouths
speaking English.

Up-close heads
with hay hair,
talk-talking,
looking right at us,
somehow seeing
past the gleaming screen
that covers the whole front
of the big flicker box.

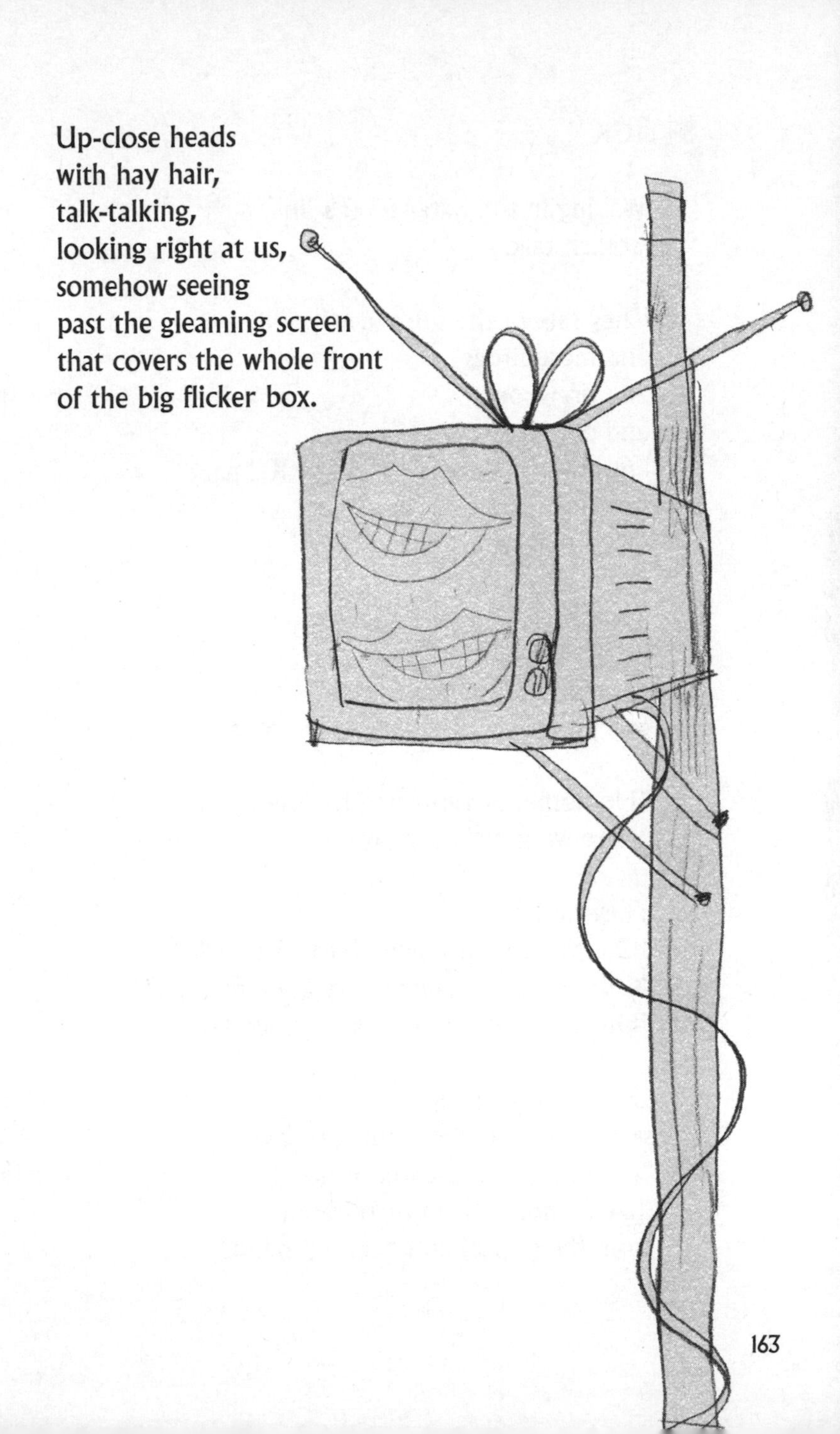

STUCK

Waiting in the water giver's line,
women talk.

They talk of the sun's heat,
and mosquitoes
and firewood
and onions,
and the everywhere bodies at Kalma,
more of them each day,
filling this camp.

They never talk of tomorrow
or any day after this one,
or what will happen to the
everywhere bodies once they come.

"No home for returning to," they say.
"Here we stay," they say.

They say:
"Our villages have been burned to ash."
"Our crops and animals are gone forever."
"Our farms, no more than memories."

One elder woman,
skin deeply creased with age, says,
"Kalma is a sharp-eared wolf
that cannot be held or released
from the grip of an uncertain hand."

Some give this elder woman
the courtesy of their attention.

Others turn their backs.
They don't want to know
what they already know.

This woman is as talky-talk as the flicker box.
"Living in a camp binds every part of us," she says.

"You cannot leave,
and you cannot enter.
Either way,
the wolf could bite you," she says.

She explains,
if someone
unrecognized
wants to come inside Kalma's boundaries,
they risk being harmed
by guards who patrol,
and ask,
"What is your purpose?"

Even when your reasons are
good and right,
you could meet trouble if the guard
thinks differently.

Other elders join in.

They say:
"The one who leaves does not return."

And:
"We cannot go back to life as it was."

They say:
"It is dangerous beyond this place."

And:
"The Janjaweed lurks. Wild hyenas wait. "

They say:
"Fat-tailed scorpions want human food."

Even though
this is what they
say,
my heart asks:

"What else *is possible?"*

FLOWERS

On gateposts, they grow.
Sprout from anything
thorny
that will let them cling.

Sudanese flowers.

They come in all colors:
white,
green,
red,
yellow,
even black.

So light,
like feathers,
these bountiful blooms.

Sudanese flowers.

When a breeze snatches one up,
it blows
along the road,
tumbling,
bouncing,
catching the toes
of a child who kicks it away.

Sudanese flowers.

They pop up everywhere at Kalma.

You can pick them,
collect them,
carry them home.

No matter the season,
they keep blooming.

They don't even need water.

These flowers,
so pretty
for anyone who finds beauty
in crumpled plastic trash bags,
    rustling,
    crinkling,
    snapping
    as they clutter our paths
    in a garbage parade.

Sudanese flowers:
trash-bag scraps
littering
our
lives.

BLOWING SMOKE

There is a girl, older than me,
but still a child.

There is a man,
older than the girl,
leading her around like she's his lamb.

Muma sees me watching.
"Her husband," she says.

The man,
her husband, is smoking a cigarette,
letting its haze form a veil
over the girl's gaze.

Doesn't he see his wife wince?

Does he hear her cough
when he flicks off the final ash,
then hurls
the brown, smoked-down butt?

The still-lit stub
lands at the front of her *toob*,
then drops.

The man summons his saliva,
spits a stream.

How rude!

NONSTOP

The flicker box never sleeps.
It's lit all day and night.

Pictures play
behind its screen.
Today someone has made it go silent.

The flicker box is on.
The flicker box is alive.

The eyes
that look out
can see.

But there's no sound
coming out
from the flicker box.

Everything is trapped
inside the flicker box.

I wonder if those hay-haired people
with big teeth and pink skin
feel the same as me:

Shut in
behind their own
mounds of sound
that can't come out.

MOON-TIME TERRORS

Leila wakes with a whimper.
She trembles,
stretches her warped limbs,
aching to make them longer.

Her spine
curls in on itself,
the stem of a gourd.

"They're back again," she cries.
"Moon-time terrors."

It's still the deepest part of night.
If only dawn were coming sooner.
Leila could watch
for the promise
of sun.

But I can tell by the mottled hunk of butter
in that high place,
and by the sky's ebony cape,
that we must endure
more darkness.

UNWELCOME

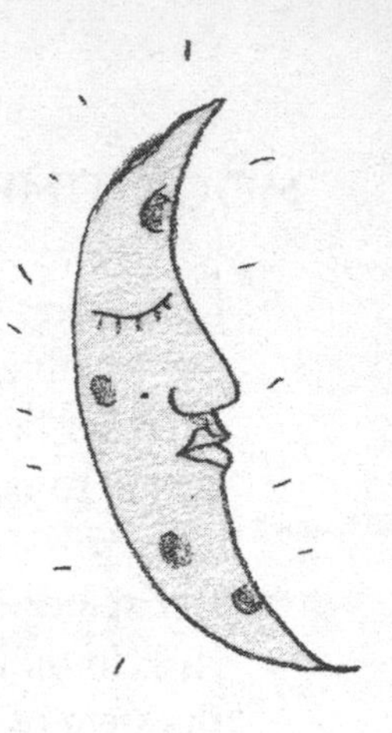

Sayidda Moon's single eye
shines brightly.

Though our village tradition tells us
the moon's fullness
is a blessing—
that her proud-lady moon face,
none of it hiding,
is good—
at Kalma,
our customs have become
a muddied swamp
of rituals from
tribes and villages
throughout Sudan.

Our beliefs about *Sayidda* Moon's power
have been stripped of their meaning,
smacked off
by heartache's hand.

Tonight the full moon
is unwelcome.

Her light,
piercing the dark,
burns a hole
through any chance for peaceful sleep.

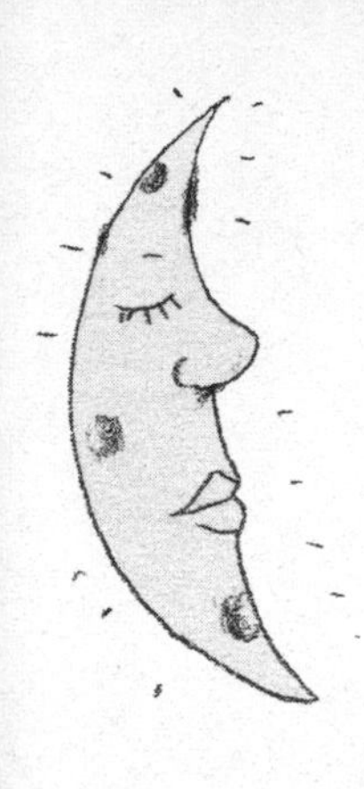

The sky ball's flash
of white
makes Leila's bad dreams
brighter.

"Make them go!"

Leila's cries bring Muma,
who settles next to my sister,
hums quietly,
rocks her crooked-limbed girl.

Leila starts to sleep
as her evil dreams flee
through the open eyelid,
ragged hole
that lets in the night's only light.

GAMAL'S GRIEF

At Kalma,
Gamal misbehaves
more than before.

He is often two ways at once.

On the edge of picking a fight,
but also ready to play.

Today he's found a bike tire,
turned it into a Hula-Hoop.

Circles it 'round
his bony-boy hips,
showing other kids how.

But then he goes from fun to mean.
When another boy wants
to give the bike-tire Hula-Hoop a try,
Gamal plays a trick.
Hurts him.

Instead of securing the rubber ring
at the boy's waist,
Gamal,
with two hands,
jams
the white-rimmed circle around the
boy's neck—and yanks it!

When the child shouts,
and calls for his mother,
Gamal is the one who starts to cry,
then speeds off screaming,
wounded.

TANTRUM

"Amira, talk!"

Gamal stamps his foot.
"Talk!"

I wish I could
just *talk.*

Gamal,
impatient,
throwing a fit.

The burn welts on his neck
have turned to pocked, blotchy scabs.
Dried citrus skin on a little kid.

He brings his face right up to mine,
shoves me with his shoulder.

As hard as I *t-r-r-r-y-y-y,*
my voice won't come.
Not even to push off Gamal.

My whole throat—pinched.
Tightly tied.

I work
to fight
the knot

pushing,
pressing,
pump-pumping
snarled air
from deep inside
my belly's belly.

No use.
No sound.

Both Gamal's feet start up in a protest.
Stomp-stomp!
Stomp-stomp!

Old Anwar,
passing by,
sees.

Rushes up,
holds Gamal firmly from behind,
pins this boy,
who is bucking.

Gamal's whole body,
stiff.
"She won't talk!"

Old Anwar says,
"Leave Amira alone.
She will speak when she's ready."

Gamal surrenders
to Old Anwar's hold,
loosens.

Old Anwar says,
"Boy child, if you must hear talking,
if you must stomp with both feet,
come with me.
We'll march to the prayer tent
and talk to Allah."

MISS SABINE

She arrives with two sacks,
oddly shaped,
hoisted on slim shoulders.

A melon-sized pouch,
filled with lots of something,
rattles from inside.
The other bag is flat, stiff, hard-edged.

This lady's *toob*,
so beautiful.
A shock of hot purple
surrounding freckled ginger skin.

She sees me looking,
not once blinking,
as she walks up to the flap
that shields the entrance of
our prayer tent.

My gaze will not leave
that rattly pouch,
or that flat bag.

Mostly, though,
something makes me
want to see what's inside
the clattering sack.

She's wearing a medallion,
this lady—
SUDAN RELIEF—
telling us
she's a visitor to Kalma.

Next to her is an intake officer,
also watching the lady's strange things.

"My name is Miss Sabine,"
says the lady with the shock-purple *toob.*

Miss Sabine's hair:
braided ropes
spilling,
blowing out
from both sides of her *toob*'s
hooded cover.

Miss Sabine's eyes:
light,
the color of sand,
flecked
with green glints.

Starshine,
those eyes.

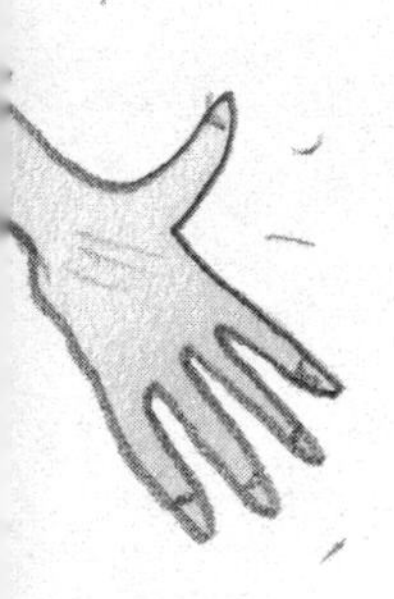

WANT

A bouquet of curious faces,
some dusty,
some polished
with sesame oil.

Girls and boys
crowd to meet Miss Sabine.

Elbows, shoulders,
poke-poking,
shove-shoving.

Wanting.

KNOWING

Leila is in the bunch,
her elbows the sharpest of all.

Her tiny limbs
weaving the slimmest spaces.

She's the first to reach Miss Sabine.
She taps at the rattly bag,
plays with it.

The intake worker presses Leila back.
"Wait," he tells her. "This lady has traveled all the way from Khartoum, Sudan's capital."

Miss Sabine lets my sister enjoy
the strangeness of her pouch,
the odd
flatness of her bag.

Leila shakes both Miss Sabine's hands,
meeting her properly.

The other girls and boys follow.
"Welcome, lady."

"*Shukran*, thank you."
Miss Sabine speaks beautifully,
in a voice that is
spice and sweet
at the same time.

I hang away from the group.
I let them move ahead.
I watch.

Miss Sabine sees me right away,
picks me out
among the many children at Kalma.

Her *goz*-colored eyes land
on me.

There is knowing
in those starshine eyes.

Miss Sabine.
Filled with understanding.

She doesn't try to make me speak.
This lady lets my silence be.

Miss Sabine.
Sudan Relief.

THE RED PENCIL

She kneels,
wriggles free
from the pouch at her back,
loosening its straps.

Then—
in one fast snap,
Miss Sabine flips the clanking bag
upside down.

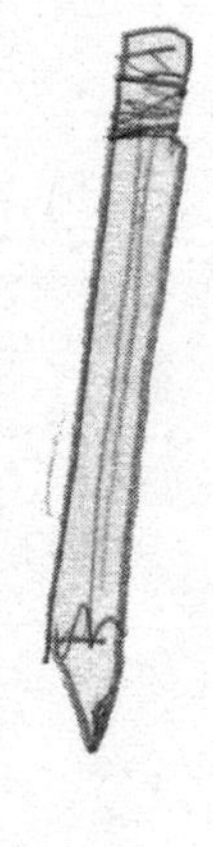

And then—
out from its drawstring mouth
spills a clattering bunch of pencils,
a yellow-coated cluster
of writing sticks
with sharpened charcoal tips!

All the children scramble,
grab,
reach.

I blink.

I want one, but I'm too slow.

Right away, the yellow sticks
are gone.

I've never left Miss Sabine's sight.

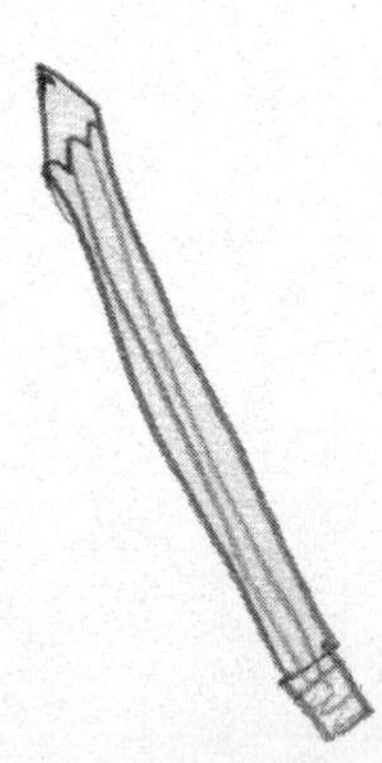

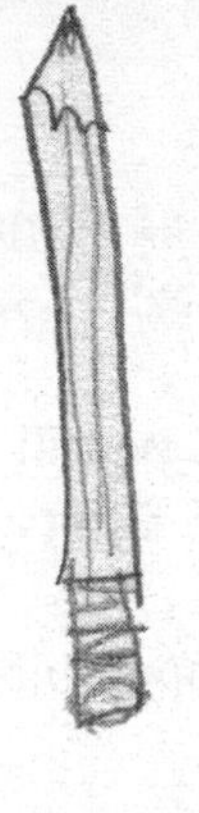

She reaches over the other children
to me,
presses a pencil into my hand.

Curls my fingers
around its middle.

"Yours," Miss Sabine says,
all with that knowing.

I'm quick to thank her
with a slight bow.

Thankfulness
wraps me
so firmly in its palm,
that I don't truly see what I'm holding.

Then—
I look.

My pencil is not like the others.
I have a *red* pencil!

And,
there is more from Miss Sabine.

She reaches deep
inside the second sack
to slide out a stack
of paper tablets.

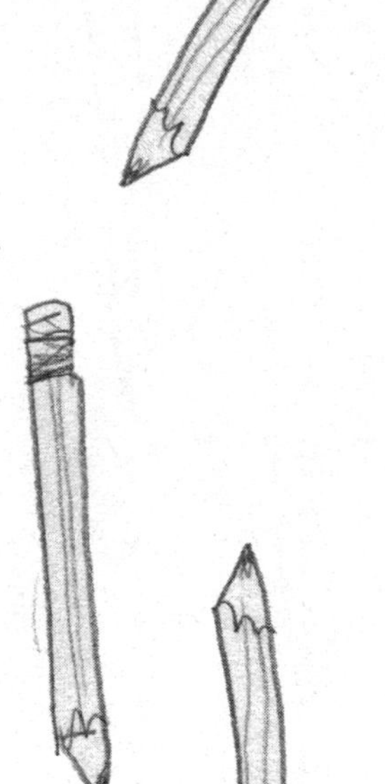

Paper as bright as our farm's wheat
in a healthy season.

A red pencil!
Yellow sheets for writing!

A happy quick-beat drums in me,
deep.

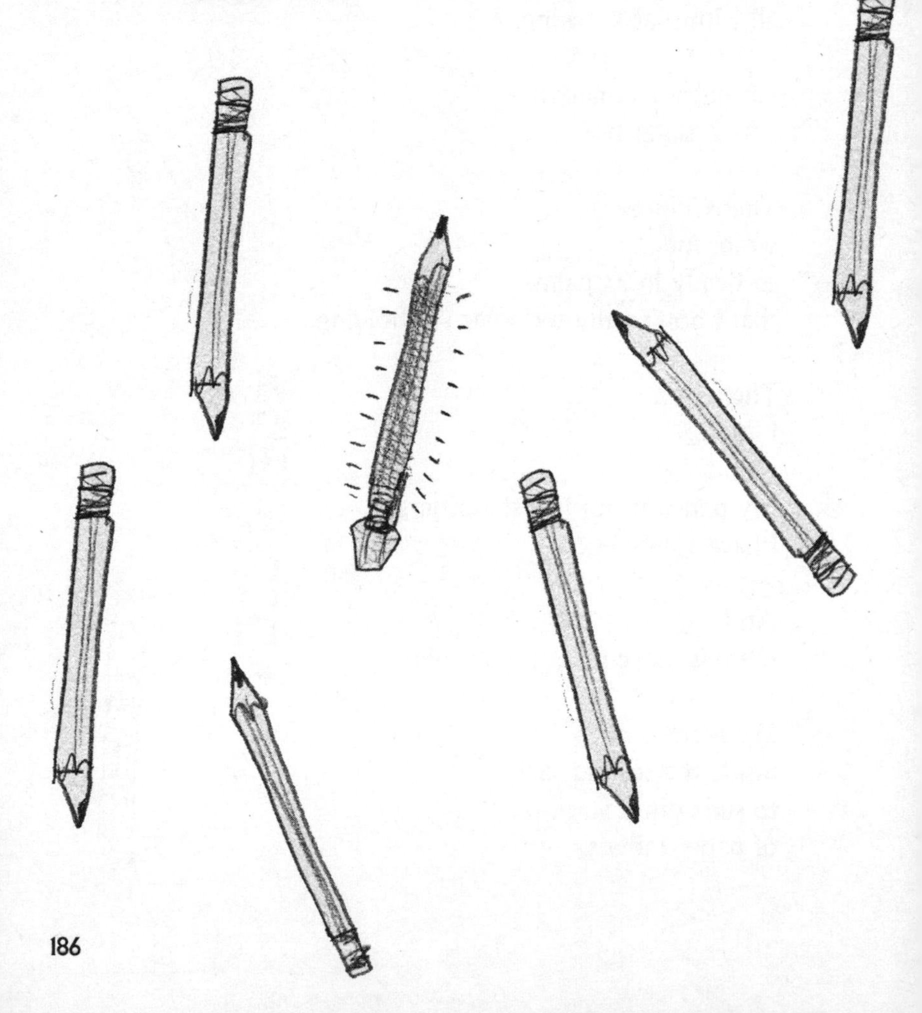

PARTING GLANCE

Miss Sabine gathers her pouches,
now empty.

The children are busy,
fanning their tablets,
playing with pencils.

This ginger-skinned lady glances at me,
her starshine eyes warm with kindness,
with encouragement.
With permission.

When the intake man escorts Miss Sabine away,
I say good-bye with a single wave,
wishing she would stay forever.

Next to Miss Sabine's
lean elegance,
the intake man
is a bloated goat.

A safari suit with many pockets
is too tight
for his squat body.

Green-dark sunglasses
mask his eyes.

STRAIGHT AND SHINY

Something about the red pencil
begs me to hold it tightly.

When I do,
it feels strange
between my thumb
and three of my fingers.

It's nothing like my twig.

It's straight and shiny,
and short.

I press its pointed end
to the yellow tablet's
paper face.

The pencil is not only red
on the outside.
It's red inside, too!

I force a mark
no bigger than the
skin crease in my bent fingers
that grip this strange,
shiny,
pointed thing that is not a twig.

The red half-a-dash
I've struck on the page
is enough drawing for
today.

I do not like this pencil.
I thought I would,
but somehow
I don't.

This pencil is hard to hold,
and much too skinny.

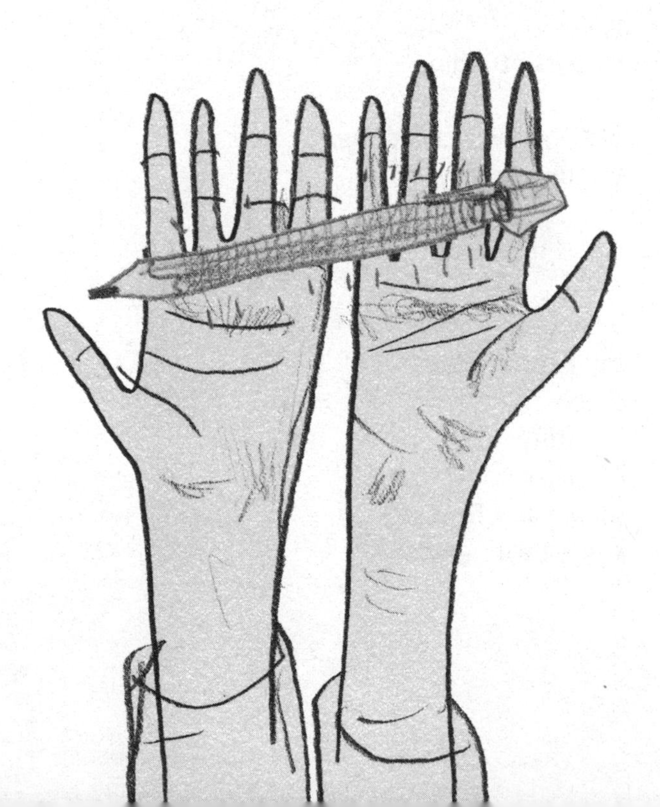

BLOCKED

My pencil tries to draw
what I remember of Nali.

But something in me
will not let
the red
shape her face,
ears,
nose.

Nali's nose.
Always nuzzling me at night,
always waking me,
warm
with its prodding.

Nali, always tickling me,
wanting to play.

This I miss most about Nali.

Why can't I make
my pencil
shape
a picture
of Nali's body,
plump as a feed sack
stuffed with grain?

OLD ANWAR'S LAMENT

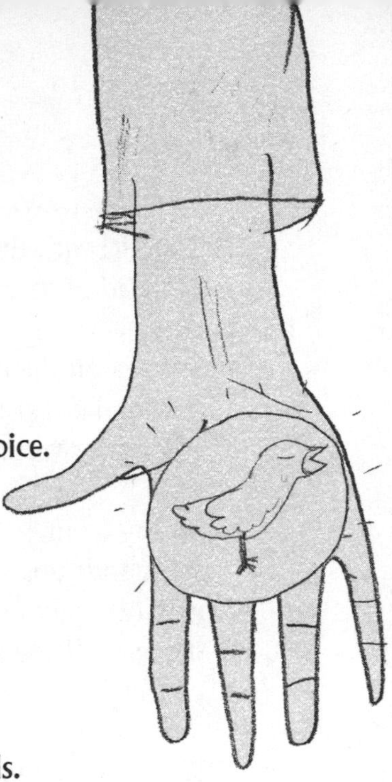

He speaks to me gently,
as if I'm his baby lamb.

"Precious Amira,
if I could,
I would chase off the pain
that has robbed your beautiful voice.

"I would replace the missing part
that has fallen from your heart.

"I would pull your voice
from inside my pocket,
lift it out,
present it to you with open hands.

"If I could,
I would stitch
that missing patch
back to your very essence.

"I would sprinkle magic *goz*
to summon your speaking.

"Precious Amira,
if I could,
I would mend
what has been snipped
from your soul."

Old Anwar, if only you could.

WIFE

The girl with the rude husband
is ahead of us in the water line.

She sits on the ground,
waiting her turn,
edging forward.

At the front,
she stands up,
gets two gallons,
trudges off the line,
panting.

Later, women gather to wash clothes.
I'm helping Muma.

The girl
is holding up a man's wet underpants.
They are stained
with what looks like remnants
of smeared plop.

She pounds at the plop with a rock.
Wrings out the underpants,
sets them on a mat to dry.

Muma says,
"That is a wife's love."

There is nothing to love about a rude man's plop.

INSIDE THE FLICKER BOX

Leila's bad dreams
and Gamal's grief
have rubbed their anguish
onto me.

Now *I* am the one
overcome.

I wake,
chilled,
even though the night is warm.

My mind
is filled with
demon dreams
of the flicker box.

The teethy people
inside that loud,
lighted thing
are trying to
bite my knuckles!

Halima is there, too,
inside the flicker box,
smiling,
waving fast,
so glad to see me!

I shimmy high up
on the pole where
the flicker box lives.

Tear off the front
of the flicker-box face.

Climb inside.
Hug Halima.

We play dizzy donkey!

We talk, talk, talk,
and sing,
and spin all day.

STIRRING A POT

Old Anwar has found a wheelbarrow
for collecting firewood.

Its hinges are rusted,
creaking a tired groan.

He's loaded the wheelbarrow's
dented well with a teetering mound
of split-open logs.

The sure hands
of this old man
prepare a cooking pit
for stirring a pot.

Our meal is a makeshift mix
of greens,
salt,
rice,
and onions,
going stale.

Old Anwar boils and sips from
a warped spoon.

His cook's flame
licks the bottom
of the pot,
set in the center of
our tiny dome-home.

Old Anwar has enhanced
the meal with lentils.

Old Anwar gathers us.
We pray,
then eat.

We scoop with
cupped fingers,
holding crusts of bread.

The food is good,
soothing.

It is made tasty
by Old Anwar's proclamation:

"We are now a family."

NEEDLE NOSES

They are quick.
They stick
to the too-small net
that does not stretch far enough
to fully protect us
from their needle noses.

For them,
this is a party.

They are gathered
and glued to the sheer,
flimsy veil.

I tuck the net in at each rice-bag corner,
pin its open flaps to the sand
with flat stones.

I might as well be trying to cover
the whole desert
with my foot's shadow.

Their celebration continues
as dusk brings more hungry guests
who slip under,
around,
in.

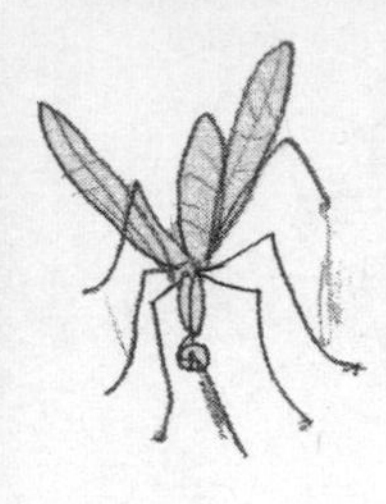

Now the fun really begins—for them.

For us, it's a fight.
Swatting!
Whacking!

Bothered by these pests, now singing.

Vzzzz-vzzzz-vzzzz!!!

Needle noses want one thing—
our warm blood.

For them,
our blood is delicious juice.

As much as we swat
and fling,
they still win.

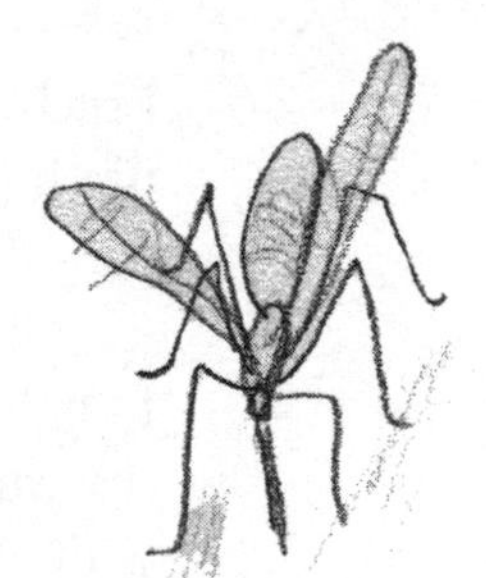

Leaving itchy welts
in their wake.

Leaving us swollen
and scratching
all night long.

For them,
paradise!

Why did Allah make mosquitoes?

SESAME OIL

Every mosquito
in all of Sudan
must be rejoicing today.

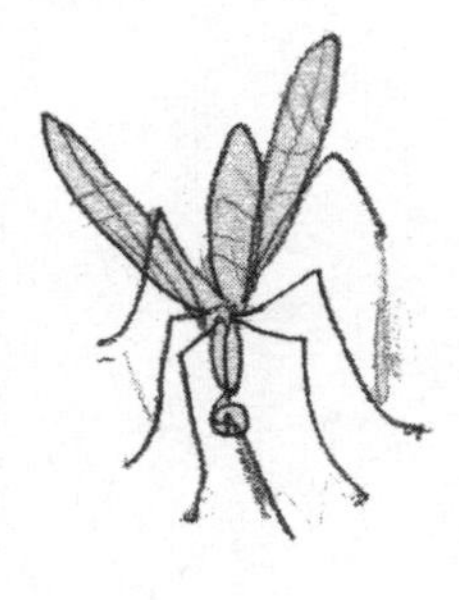

Their blood-sucking party
was a grand celebration.

Muma slathers me,
Leila,
and Gamal
with sticky sesame oil.

"It will keep mosquitoes away,"
she claims.

I hope she's right.

Those pointy-nosed pests
have blotched my skin
with their ugly designs.

This is why
I let Muma
turn me
into a greased girl.

QUESTIONS

My voice,
still silenced,
is buried.

Still, I do not speak.
Still, I cannot speak.

Yet,
there are many questions
I want to ask my mother.

But I do not ask.
I cannot ask.

Perhaps it is good
that I do not,
cannot.

My questions would vex Muma.

Yet,
I want to ask my mother
why she bothers to sweep
the dirt floor
of our dirty hut.

I want to ask my mother
what she prays for each morning,
and at dusk.

I want to ask my mother
if she saw my father fall.

There are so many questions
I do not,
cannot,
ask my mother.

I do not
want to vex my mother.

NEW NEIGHBOR

Who are you, bushy bundle?

Waddling with a will
through the crevice
that separates our hut
from the one next door.

I see you nosing your way
past trash
and dirt-caked paths
that have carved themselves
between
half-baked homes,
hungry
for anything
that will change them
from makeshift
to livable.

Bushy bundle,
what brings you here
to the cruddy gutters
of Kalma?

I never saw a creature
like you on our village farm.

It's only when Old Anwar
spots your waddle
that I learn of the proper name
chosen for you by Allah,
when the Almighty was molding creatures.

Old Anwar greets you with
the same respect
he shows all living things.

He bows to address you.

"Hello, hedgehog."

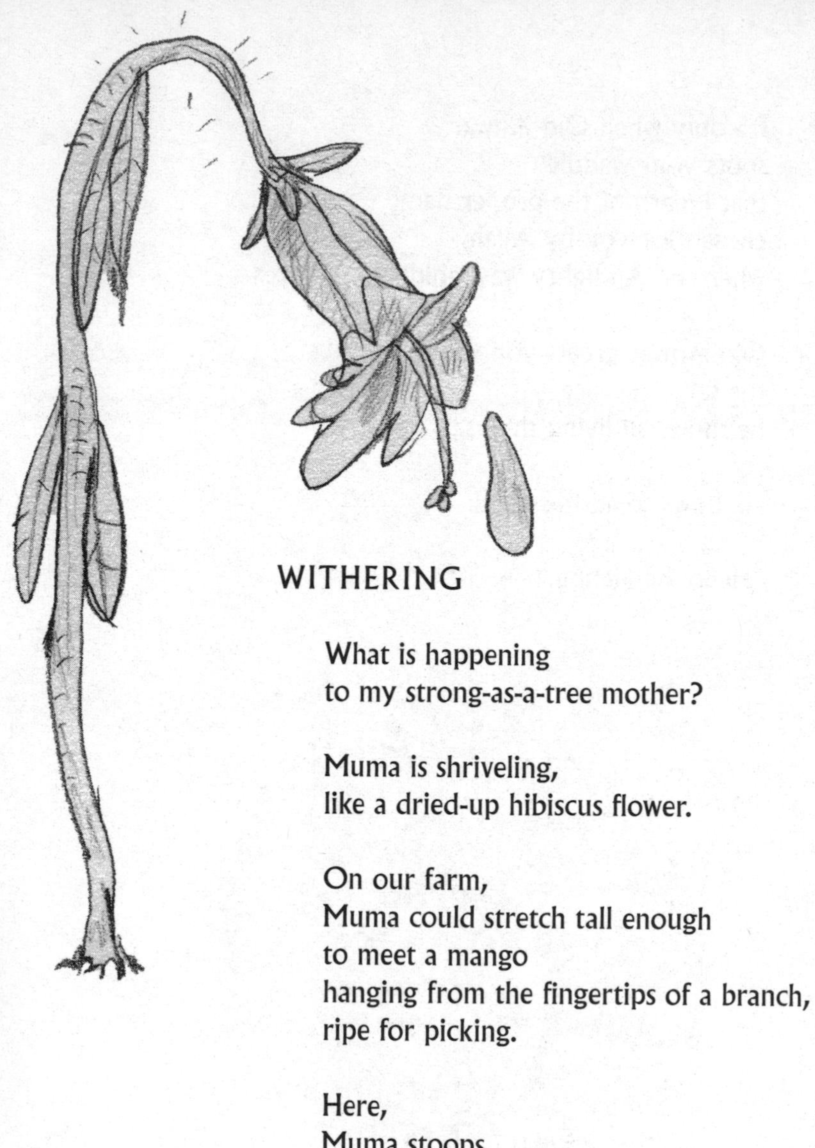

WITHERING

What is happening
to my strong-as-a-tree mother?

Muma is shriveling,
like a dried-up hibiscus flower.

On our farm,
Muma could stretch tall enough
to meet a mango
hanging from the fingertips of a branch,
ripe for picking.

Here,
Muma stoops.

Here,
she has nothing to reach for.

SAD-QUIET

Leila's new ditty
is a tinny whisper.

"My sister can't sing.
My sister can't shout.

My sister's voice,
it won't come out.

My sister, so sad.
My sister, so quiet.

My sister's sad-quiet
will not go away.

My sister's sad-quiet
will not let her say,

'Sister Leila,
let's go play!'

My sister's sad-quiet
makes me sad-quiet, too."

FENCES

Who planted these blue
rows
on my yellow paper's face?

Why these lines?

They are ugly wire fences
preventing
my pencil
from roaming.

My *sparrow*
is trying to
fly,
but struggling.

She cannot
lift.

The up-jumpy bird
inside me,
the spirit-wings that soar
when I draw,
are trapped behind
these blue-bar barricades.

When the papermakers
were making paper,
did anyone ask,

Why these lines?

NO BLUE BOUNDARIES

Today the red pencil does more
than beg for my hand.

It makes me a promise.
It tells me to try.

Ignore these blue lines.
Just draw.

This pencil
must somehow know
that by gripping tightly,
while letting it wander,
I can free the pictures
raging through my memory.

AWAKENED

Today my *sparrow* starts to flutter.

My soul's bird wakes,
calling me
to draw
a wicked helicopter
with the face of a camel,
spitting big bullets.

Below are tiny people,
powerless.

Running for cover
like ants in a rainstorm.

Dando is among them,
dying.

DRENCHED

A downpour
of bloodshed,
falling fast,
like rain,
after bullets fly.

Dot! *Dot!*
Dot! *Dot!*
Dot.
Dot! *Dot!*
Dot!
Dot!
Dot! *Dot!* *Dot!*
Dot!
Dot! *Dot!* *Dot!*

Dot! *Dot!*
Dot!
Dot!
Dot! *Dot!*
Dot! *Dot!*
Dot!

Dot!
Dot! *Dot!*

LISTENING

There's a distant call,
something muffled,
coming from a locked place.

It's bumping against
the sides of a box,
wanting to be freed.

*Ya...ya...*it tells me.

Listen.

The voice is a little bit familiar.

But still, I must strain to
fully make it out.

Ya...ya...ya...

My pencil helps.

It crafts the sound.

Ya...ya...
the pencil's music.

It plays on paper,
shows me highs,
lows,
in-betweens.

Ya...ya...
my pencil sings.

My *sparrow* springs!

A quick-rush—*ya...ya.*

Suddenly I see.
Suddenly—*ya...ya*—I hear
clearly.

The muffled,
bumping,
more-faint-than-a-whisper,
aching-for-sound,
is *me,*
preparing to speak.

FREEING MUMA

Another night of Muma's silent pain.

This time I won't let her cry alone.
I can't do that to Muma.
It's cruel to ignore her.
It's unkind to pretend I don't hear my mother aching.

I know Muma wishes I didn't see her
when she weeps.

But too bad.
She'll just have to face the shame.

I go to her pallet,
gently put both hands at her back.

Muma sits up quickly,
turns to me,
her eyes tired.

Then it happens.
It happens to me.
It happens to Muma.

With a force all its own,
it happens.

Like the *haboob*, we can't stop it.
We can't run away.
It's here.

A thick moan
rolls out from deep places.

It's the same for each of us,
but different, too.

Muma's is heavy,
pounding
like so much wind from the *haboob*.

Mine breaks through a cracked patch
in my throat,
then rips through all of me—
thundering.

RELEASE

For the first time since Dando died.
For the first time since we left our farm.
For the first time in a long time,
        Muma and I hold each other.

        And cry.
        Together.

Muma's arms,
folded around me,
so feeble.

All of her is shaking,
like from a fever.

Both our faces,
wet.

Tears,
on our chins,
on our necks.

Soaking the fabric
of our wrinkled cottons.

My arms,
small beneath Muma's
but strong enough to show my mother
she's allowed to cry.

Now,
after so much time
traveling through dry sand.

Now,
after so much walking among brittle dirt.

Now,
after working hard,
like camels,
to store all that's inside,

Muma and I
surrender to something
we've fought
to hold off.

Knowing that if we let it begin,
we may never stop.

Here comes gut-sound,
starting slow,
building,
then melting to shuddered breaths.

Until,
finally,
we sleep.

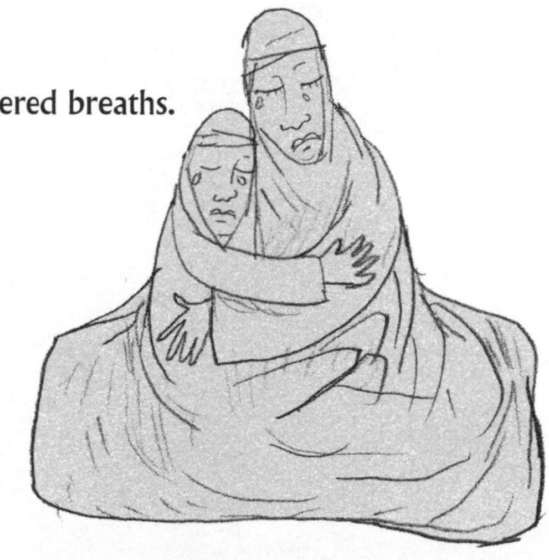

HEALING

I show Old Anwar my red pencil.
"It suits you," he says.
"Such a bold color. Strong."

I share my drawings.
Old Anwar looks
closely.

"Healing" is all he says.

COULD IT BE?

My pencil and tablet are gone
from the tucked-under place
beneath my pallet!

I have lost so much!

It's hard to ask
What else is possible?

I don't want to work
at coming up with
It could be.

The game doesn't work right now!

I rifle through the folds of the
two *toobs* I own.

I search every reed
that forms my pallet,
praying my pencil is somehow
stuck between.

Hoping my tablet has slipped,
and was kicked
by unknowing feet
to someone else's sleeping spot.

All day there's a thump
pounding hard through every part of me.

I reverse *It could be…*
to *Could it be?…*

Could it be that I'm somehow
a cursed girl
who loses everything she loves?

By evening, I've given up.

But there's good in this defeat.
It brings back my voice,
full-on.

ROAR!

First, grunts.

Then,
it's a friend,
returning,
speaking up,
shouting out,
for me:

"My. Red. Pencil!"

I find an abandoned shanty,
where I can let go.

It's dark when I enter.
I hear soft humming.
I lift my lantern.

Leila!

She's hidden in a dusty corner.
Her cheeks glisten like lighted fruits.
Her hum-hum is happy.
She's with Gamal.

They have my red pencil
and my paper tablet.

Leila can barely grip the pencil,
but when Gamal's hand guides hers,
her fingers work.

Both their faces
are filled with determination.

They're taking turns,
scribbling.

A breath storms through me,
rasping,
fierce.

I roar,
"Give. Me. My. Red. Pencil!"

I've startled Leila.
Gamal, too.

My sister sucks in a breath.
Her eyes are brimming
with giddy surprise.
"Amira!"

Gamal gently nudges Leila with his shoulder.
A smirk plays on his face.

He looks pleased,
relieved.

A lively frog,
ready to jump at some fun.

Gamal has gone from greedy
to glad.

He thrusts my straight-and-shiny friend
right under my nose.

"Amira, here's your pencil back!"

ERASE

At the red pencil's end
stands a hard lump of clay.
I do not like its green.
So ugly, its green.

And pointy.

A baby snake's head.
A thistle's pricker.

A sick fish,
this green.

My speaking is still in snippets.

I ask Old Anwar,
"What to do with this clump?"

He tries to explain.
"An eraser."

He shows me how
the baby snake's head
can fade the red's bright lines,
leaving smears
on the yellow page,
and green dust in its wake.

“Erase,” he says.
“Why erase?” I ask.
“For mistakes,” he says,
still trying to explain.

Mistakes?
My sparrow
sees no mistakes.

My sparrow *sees only what*
it sees.

Erase?

To me,
that is the mistake—to erase.

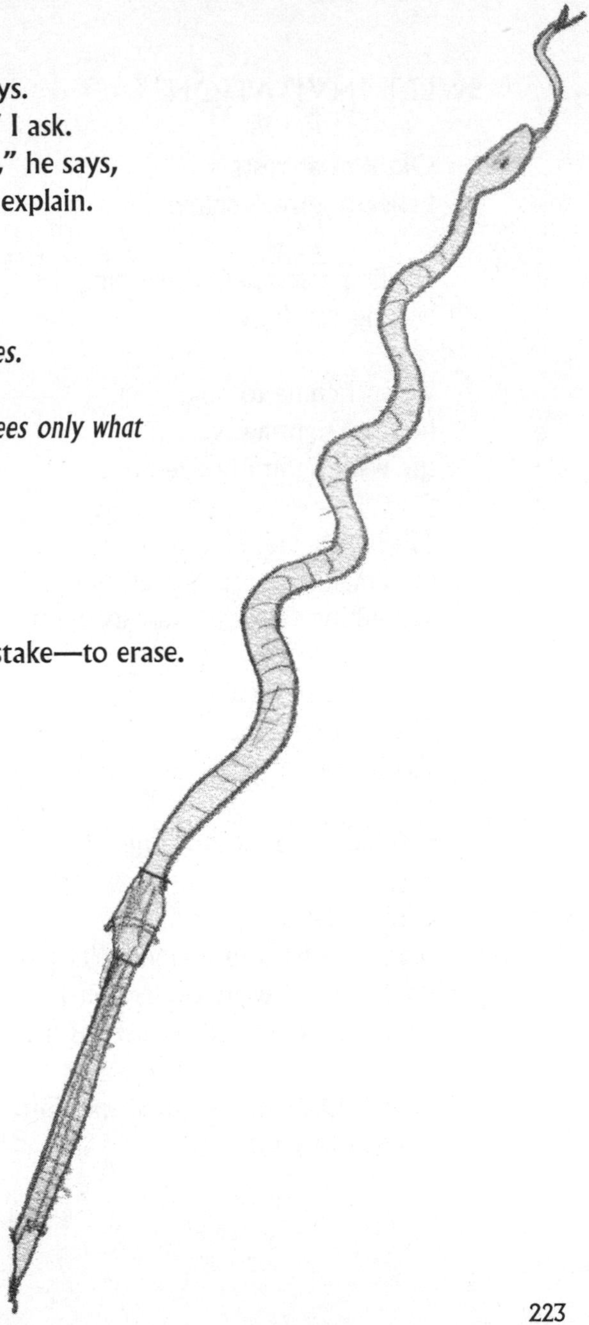

SWEET INVITATION

Old Anwar rests
beneath a tree's shade.

His finger scrapes at dry dirt,
writing carefully.

When I come to him,
he sees, right away,
the wanting in my eyes.

"Sit beside me, Amira.
I am making a list of gratitude.
Something I do each day as the sun sets."

A distant bird calls.
Then crickets.
Toads, too.

Evening's celebration song.

Old Anwar says,
"Land has its own memory, its own power.
That is why I write on its tablet.
To press life into what sustains us."

I watch Old Anwar put shapes into crusted soil,
crafting beauty.

My eyes are afraid to blink.
I don't want to miss a single bit of Old Anwar's
soil writing.

"*I* want to learn letters," I blurt.

Old Anwar is silent, thinking.

Quietly, he says,
"Amira, there is talk
of creating a full school at Kalma.
Until it is here, *I* will teach you."

I lower my head. "Muma will never allow it."

I explain Muma's warning about chasing the wind.

Old Anwar lifts my chin.
"I will instruct you in secret.
At night, by lantern.
Muma will never know of it."

Old Anwar's promise,
it is a sweet invitation.
"But what of Muma's warning?" I ask.

Old Anwar says,
"Amira, you are not *chasing* the wind.
You are stirring it up."

TO...

To craft letters.
To see reading's beauty.
To write English.
To recite the Koran, our holy book.
To know reading's music.

To me, these are wondrous
treasures.

MY A

Old Anwar wraps his knobby fingers
around my hand.
Guides my finger,
helps me write.

He shows me
that in the English alphabet
his name and mine
begin the same—with an *A*.

"Now you," he encourages,
watching the soil
as I slice its surface
to form the English alphabet symbol
that starts my name.

It's a strong, handsome character,
this English-alphabet *A*.

My finger strikes two lean,
angled lines,
pressed
forehead to forehead
and holding hands.

I make this *A*
with my own special stroke.

My A
has long legs
that walk forward on the sand.

My A
marches past anything
that dares to block it.

Old Anwar purses his crinkled lips
into a smile that can only mean
satisfaction.

"Your hand already understands
that writing letters
and drawing are the same," he says.
"Letters are pictures that make words."

I see what Old Anwar means.

My A
lets me feel the truth
of what he's saying.

But still, to be certain, I ask,
"That is all there is *to* it?"

Old Anwar's nod
shows me:
Yes!

MATHEMATICS

Old Anwar likes arithmetic.
He demonstrates a simple equation:

1 + 1 = two hands full.
An onion in my right.
Stone in my left.

I do not like filled-up hands.

This counting,
and holding on,
prevents me from writing.

Old Anwar tries to make me see differently.
"You are adding up Allah's abundance," he says.

I set the onion and the stone at Old Anwar's feet.
"Arithmetic is not for me."

I slide my pencil from a knotted tether
at the base of my *toob*,
settle my tablet on my lap, then quick-swirl shapes
to make an onion-stone necklace.

This math lesson has multiplied my desire to draw.

FUNNY BUGS

Old Anwar says,
"Practice puts a shine on the mind."

We continue with lessons,
each night,
working to shine
what is becoming my own precious jewel.

The two of us meet in the empty shanty
where Leila and Gamal
shared my pencil and tablet.

Old Anwar insists
I learn more letters
from the English alphabet.

Strange,
this English alphabet.

The letter *A*,
that was easy.

But the English alphabet is filled with
funny bugs:

P *N* *Y* *L*
Q *G* *H*
J *R* *X*
E *S* *B* *O*
M *C* *D*

The winking light from Old Anwar's lantern makes the letters dance.

FAVORITE

Of all the funny-bug letters I know,
the letter *O*
is my favorite shape.

Ya, O!

Open.
Unbroken.
Eternal.

Ya, O!

POPULATION

This time
when we wait
in the water giver's line,
I hear one tell another about
so many thousands
living at Kalma.

That is a strange number.
So many thousands.

I try to make sense of it.

So many thousands of everywhere bodies.
So many thousands of nomads, wandering nowhere.
So many thousands, torn from tribal villages.
So many thousands of bellies, hungry for home.
So many thousands, aching for safety.
So many thousands of hearts, longing.

Here is the problem:
So many thousands of nomads + bellies +
souls + hearts + wandering + torn
+ hungry + aching + longing =
too many
tragedies
to count.

Even Old Anwar's
knack for mathematics
can't add it all up.

To me,
this is a hard lesson.

Math is useful,
but makes my head hurt.

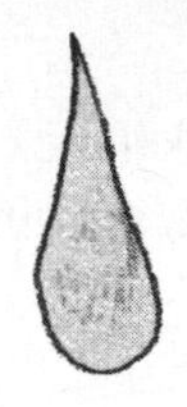

BUTTERFLIES

Gamal is quick
to show me his own sheet
of yellow-lined tablet paper.

There is a picture,
made in gray pencil.

It's of a boy
with tears as big as butterflies,
fluttering out,
parading down
from eyes shut tight.

The boy
is reaching toward clouds
shaped like a mother and a father,
his hands yearning for hugs
from heavenly parents.

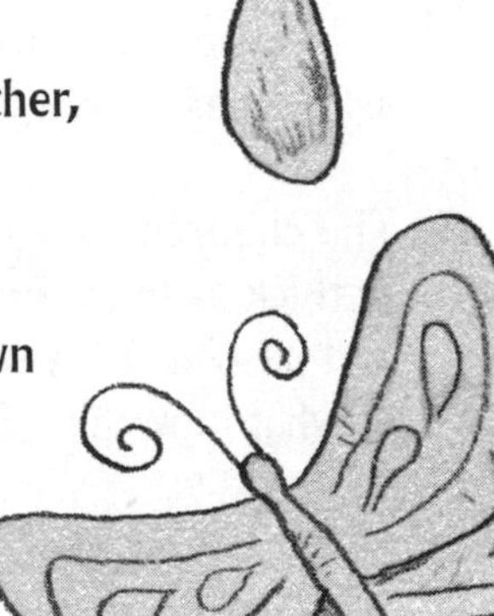

"Gamal," I ask, "*you* have drawn
this?"

He nods.

I say,
"It is a beautiful way to cry."

CNN

The flicker box makes me stop and watch.
Dancing, glowing letters:
CNN

But that's not all.
The lady inside the flicker box is speaking Arabic.
She's talking about Nyala!

There are quick-moving pictures
of Gad Primary School!

Its walls,
white bricks, and clean.

Its door,
as blue and as welcoming
as a sunrise sky.

The children have books
as thick as those bricks,
and baskets filled with pencils
of what looks like so many thousands of colors!

There are many girl students,
dressed in matching *toobs*,
and boys as young as Gamal,
in white shirts and short pants,
all crisp.

They're chanting the alphabet in English,
singing out the letters together.

They're laughing!

I look for my friend.
Halima,
are you there?

So many faces,
bright with excitement.

Reading many books!
Blessed with pencils!
Paper tablets everywhere!

Two women, writing yellow funny bugs
on big boards,
black as tar.

The students are all reading together,
out loud, for everyone to hear.

CNN, wait!
You dance too fast.

Please,
slow down.
I want to see more.

But—*pop!*—like a tooth suddenly gone,
CNN's moving pictures disappear,
drowning in a cloud of static.

SURPRISE

Old Anwar has brought a gift
wrapped in burlap.
"This," he explains,
"is Allah's strongest root.
Like you, Amira, it pushes
through the sand's grittiest surface."

I peel open the coarse fabric.
My gift is a roasted yam,
heavy, bumpy,
bigger than Old Anwar's fist.

Its skin glistens,
as if Allah's root has been polished
with enchanted oils.

"Where did you get it?" I ask.
"Taste," Old Anwar encourages,
not answering my question.

I know a yam's flavor.
I've eaten many yams
on our farm,
but none at Kalma.

I bite into the yam's
pointy top
to get at my gift's starchy insides.

Old Anwar must know his yam is magic.
"I roast it in a way no one else can.
Old Anwar's way."
The yam's flavor is a nutty burst,
slightly burned, and so, so good.

I take only one more tiny bite,
then wrap my glistening gift
to keep for later.

Old Anwar gently lifts my pencil,
smooths my yellow paper with his palm.
He writes a new English word,
tells me how to say it properly.

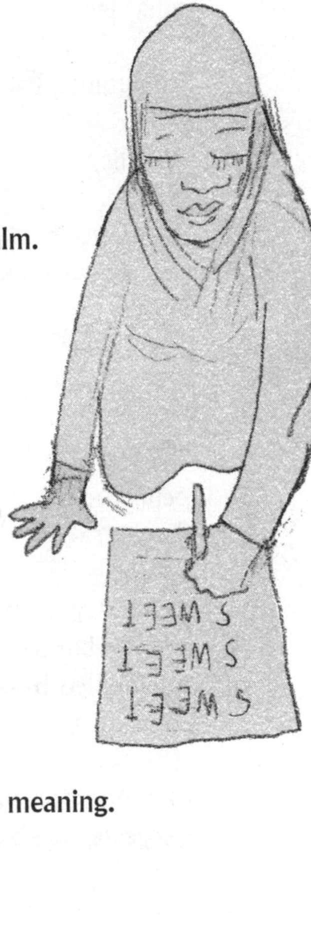

Sweet.

Slowly, I repeat.

With my pencil,
I swirl *sweet's* delicious beauty
onto my tablet's paper.
Sweet.
Sweet.
Sweet.

I have already tasted this new word's meaning.

BUSHY BUNDLE

Fat-shaped,
hairy-faced,
bushy body,
squat legs.

Soft-quilled back.

Waddle,
waddle,
taking your
own slow clumsy
stroll
anyplace
you choose.

Shading with my
pencil point's
flattest side,
I color
to make your bushy-haired,
chubby-bundle,
soft-quilled back
come alive.

One question I must ask:
Hedgehog, where do you hide your eyes?

THE FUTURE

I now know what
I want
to be.

Not a farmer.
Not a wife.
Not even a keeper of sheep.

I want
to make words,
draw slants
and dots
and circle-shapes
for others' eyes to see.

I want
to teach it all to girls and boys,
ready to read and rise.

This is what
I want.

MINE

My yam stays hidden
under the dusty,
rumpled blanket
at the foot of my pallet.

I take a tiny yam-bite each day.

Sweet.
Sweet.

Shiny-skinned magic.

I try, oh, I try,
to make my gift last.
It's not easy.

I know I should share
with Leila and Gamal,
but after only three days,
my yam is down
to a final thumbnail morsel.

There's just not enough left for sharing.

I have little choice but to keep
the sweet,
roasted bit
all for me.

SOUP-CAN SOCCER

Gamal gets there first.

His side-footed
swipe
sends the battered tin
clattering.

Even on banana legs,
Leila is just as fast,
fighting
to get the "ball"
away from Gamal.

She pings it,
pops it,
keeps it tumbling.

The "ball's" scraped label
gives a glimpse
of the soup
that once filled its belly:

ICKEN OODLE.

Leila kick-kicks
the "icken oodle"
past her opponent,
charging it

down,
down,
down,
a field of no grass,
until Leila shouts, "Goal!"

Rejoicing in her win
at one-on-one
soup-can soccer.

BRUSHING DUST

I'm ready to ask my mother
one of many vexing questions.

Muma is sweeping the dirt floor
of our rice-sack house.

So much sweeping,
always sweeping,
brushing dust
into puff-puffs
that billow
at Muma's ankles.

My words come as telling,
not as asking.

"I want to leave Kalma.
I want to go to Nyala."

Muma stoops to pick up
a stubborn pebble that will
not yield to her broom's stiff bristles.

She flings the tiny menace
to a corner,
sweeping faster,
not once looking up
from the brown dirt clouds
gusting off her hard work.

"Amira, I'm busy," she says.

HANDLEBAR HAPPY!

Gamal's spindly shins,
peddling fast
on a rickety
fender-bent bike.

He doesn't seem to notice
the sagging chain
or crooked seat,
or squeaky wheel.

Gamal is too busy
balancing
a boy on the wide-armed
handlebars.

His passenger is that same child
whose neck Gamal nearly snapped
in his moment of heated grief.

But today he's invited this kid
to ride
up front.

To be his special traveler
on a dust-powered path
at dusk
lit by glints of gold
winking from the bike's cracked
back reflector.

Gamal speeds up.
The giddy boy squeals.

Friends,
handlebar happy!

RED-EYED ROBBER

A burglar has come to my sleeping corner.
She's a sneaky thief.

I hear the tiny scuffles
her four feet make
as she rummages near my pallet.

Her whiskers twitch.

"You can't hide
in this wide-open place," I whisper.

This red-eyed rat,
this crafty criminal,
knows I've caught her
before she can even try to steal
what's mine.

She watches my yam scrap
with her red rat eyes,
hoping I won't stop her.

This red-eyed robber is stealing,
but it's hard to get angry.
She's leaving behind a gift.
She's given me a giggle.

I tell her,
"Go ahead, you sneaky thief."

Hunger won't let her wait.
She snatches up
my last bit of *sweet*
in her teeth.

Scratches at the dirt floor,
scurries.

Escapes through a slit
in the rice-bag wall,
her red-eyed robber's
safety hatch.

NEW FAMILY PICTURES

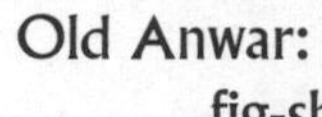

Old Anwar:
fig-shaped chin,
cheeks high,
sharp,
pushing out
from black-creased
skin.

Hatch-hatch—
quick mustache,
patched to the top
of a parched,
dark
lip.

Shoulders,
solid blades
hoisting heavy memories.

Bunions forcing his feet
into crumpled clusters
of toe bones and tight skin.

Gamal:

wide-open eyes,
smiling,
seeing possibilities
in "icken oodle"
and broken bottles.

Gapped teeth,
ready to take a bite
out of anything that
tastes like sticky
mischief.

Dusty skin,
smooth,
yet marred by
healed ropes of
burned flesh
fanning his neck.

Hair,
a rounded,
nubby
puff,
shaping
his face.

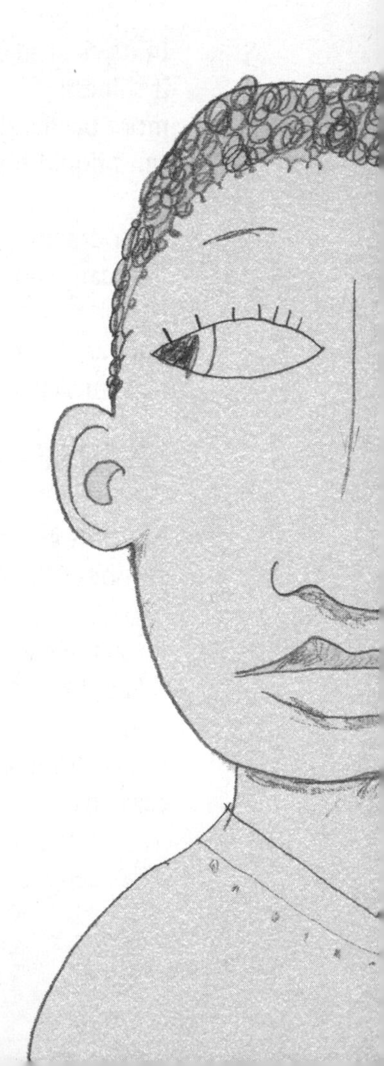

LOVE

A new treat from Old Anwar.

This one sweeter than sweet,
and brighter
than even the ripest yam.

In its clear glass bottle,
it shines
more brilliantly than the
sun's liquid heat.

It's a dream
that can come
true
only at the hands
of a miracle maker.

Orange Fanta!

My eyes go wide.
So does Old Anwar's smile.

I don't ask where
this bold
bolt
of hot-colored soda
came from.

I learned
from the yam
that Old Anwar won't tell.

He says, "Drink."

The bottle's cap
has been removed.

My dream-treat is open,
ready.

It's warm, sparkling.

I don't even care
about the family of ants
crowding at the bottle's top,
fighting to dive
inside.

I blow at the bugs,
brush clean the glass rim,
kiss that bottle right on its
lip!

Then—*ya!*

I quick-swig.
It's hard not to suck down every delicious drop.
I drink only half,
leaving some to share with Leila and Gamal.

But oh, oh, oh!
How can I not finish off this treat?

I utter a quick, silent prayer.
Allah, strengthen me.

I breathe, close my eyes.
Press back my urge to drink it all.

Take one more taste
of the orange-sweet
syrupy brew.

Fanta soda,
I love you!

GUZZLING

When I bring Gamal and Leila the Fanta,
they do something unexpected.

They don't even fight
over its bright
delight.

Gamal says, "Leila, you first."
Leila sips, then says, "Gamal, you now."

They pass the pop-treat back and forth,
licking their lips,
tasting the sweet on their teeth,
savoring.

Then Gamal and Leila grant another surprise.

They leave the final guzzle for me,
letting me hug my bottle,
not a broken dolly,
but a sugar-bright memory
of shared joy.

FANTA FLUTE

If
I shape
my lips
to make
the letter
O,
then blow
on my empty soda bottle's
O,
then—*oh!*—I have a Fanta flute.

Hooty music skims
from the glass-lipped rim:

Toot!

HALIMA, PROFILE

Red pencil, red pencil,
show me my friend.

Forehead,
rounded and proud.

Eyelash up-flips,
curly beauty.

Smile bones—strong!

The slope of her nose,
ending in a pudgy bump
that leads to full lips,
ready to say:
"Amira, come to my new school!"

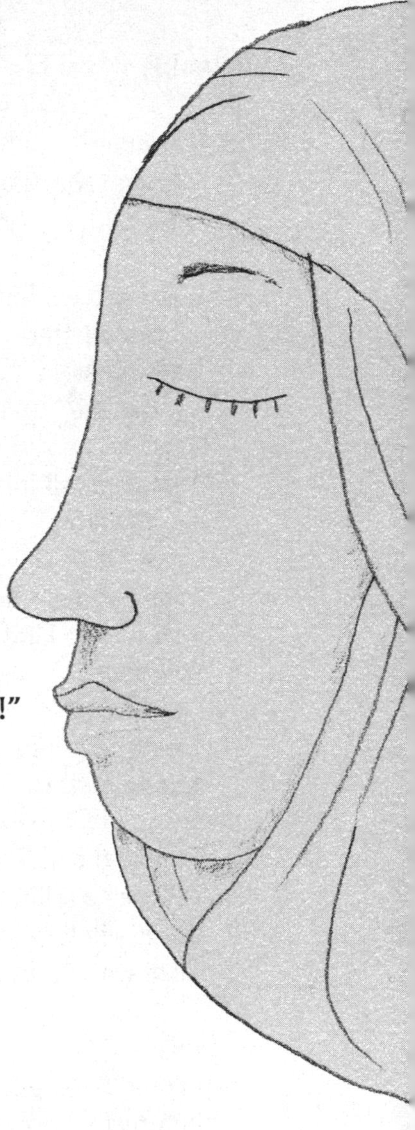

I WISH

I'm quiet
during today's lesson
with Old Anwar.

I want to tell him
learning letters
and words
pleases me.

I want to tell him
I'm thankful.

I want to tell Old Anwar
that he's so kind,
so good.

I want to tell him,
too, my wish.

I know they are trying
to make a school here at Kalma,
but it will be a rice-bag shack
filled with Sudanese flowers.

I wish
I could have lessons
in a real school,
with other girls,
with Halima.

And books
and a blackboard,
and laughing,
and many
students,
chanting,
singing,
trapping
funny-bug alphabet letters
that flit on that blackboard.

After everything he's done to teach me to read,
I can tell none of this to Old Anwar.

LEAP

"What snare has trapped you, Amira?"
Old Anwar asks.

His eyes let me know
I can trust him.

Words leap from me
like a grasshopper
freed from a folded palm.

"Gad Primary School—in Nyala," I say,
my words surging.

Old Anwar
lets my wish settle
like his tasty mixture of greens and rice.

And, like his makeshift meal,
his expression is an odd mix.

He looks pleased
and questioning,
and troubled.

I ask,
"Have I hurt you, Old Anwar?"

I can't look at him.
He's silent, folding his hands,
pressing at his knuckles.

I say,
"You have given me such good lessons.
"I should not have spoken about wishes.
I will endure a scolding."

I lower my head,
ready to accept
my reprimand.

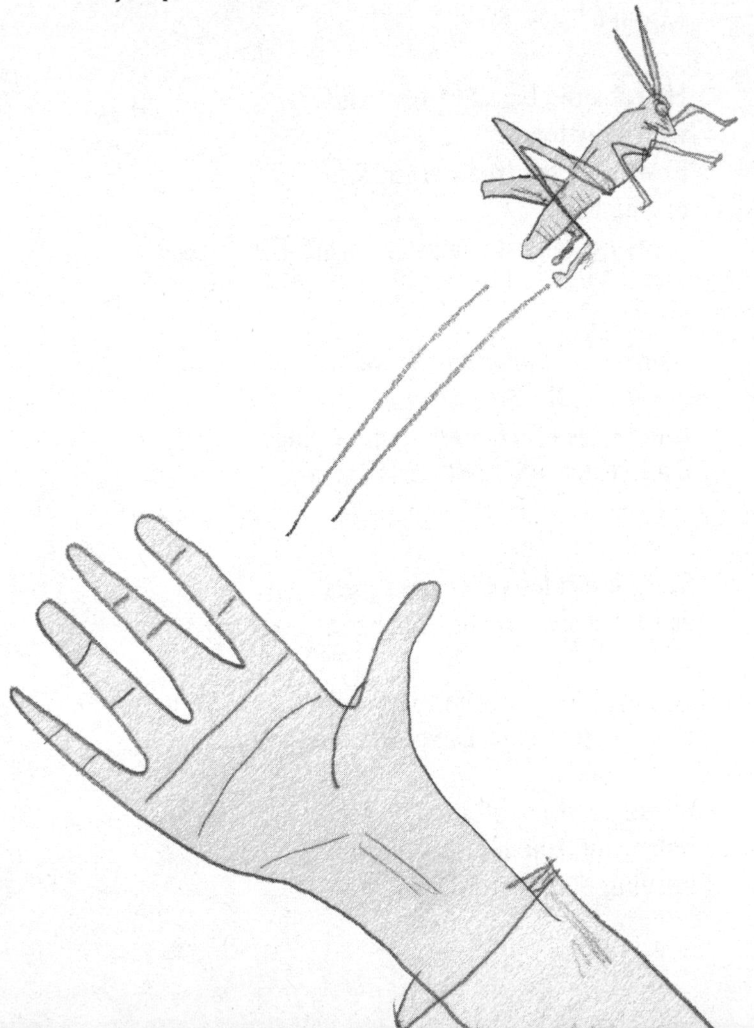

ANTHILL

Old Anwar says,
"I am the one
to be admonished
for not seeing
that the bright star right in front of me
needs a bigger sky
to shine."

He rubs the backs of his hands
with slow force.
I can hear the weathered skin
of one hand
coursing against the ashen skin of the other.

He says,
"Amira, you are right to want proper schooling,
but even Old Anwar
cannot bring this desire into being.
Gad Primary School costs money.
We do not have the means."

Scaly knuckles whisper regrets
as Old Anwar wrings his hands even harder.

He says, "And Nyala is several miles from here.
It is dangerous to travel while war rages."

I watch a circle of ants
scurrying near my toes,
pushing dirt, building a mound.

I know how those ants feel.
They're small, but want to climb the hill.
Old Anwar's discouragement
feels like a gritty-skinned heel
smashing my own hill of hope.

ENVY

I follow the hedgehog,
past gutters jammed
with orange peels,
rotting melon rinds,
and broken bottle dollies.

Sudanese flowers
float like ghosts
haunting the afternoon.

Her hidden eyes know where to look
to find the way.

She senses I'm close behind.

Her bushy bottom
toddles,
twitches a rhythm that invites me:
Come along.

We go
past trenches
dug
by worn feet
that have traveled the alleys
between so many
ugly
dome-homes.

This know-it-all hedgehog
has a plan.

We come to Kalma's intake gate,
where the stocky guard in his safari suit
and green-dark sunglasses waits,
paces.

He's busy eating peanuts,
shells and all.

He's busy drinking Fanta.
He's busy burping.

I stop.
I can go no farther
before Mr. Safari Suit questions me.

But the hedgehog,
she keeps going.

Wheedles
past dropped peanuts
and bottle caps.
Flattens her quills
—then, *fweep!*—quick-shimmies
beneath
the chain-link fence
that keeps Kalma a closed-in
trap.

I watch
the bushy bundle,
envious.

TUG-OF-WAR

Now it's Muma
and Old Anwar who are arguing.

Rice-bag walls don't allow
privacy.

I sit on a stone outside our hut,
rinsing the sheet
that rests beneath my pallet.

Old Anwar and Muma
are fighting.
Fighting about me.

Muma's words have fire on them.
"You are wasting her time!"

"*You* are wasting *her*!" Old Anwar snaps.
"There are attempts to make a school here anyway.
Soon you will not be able to prevent
what is meant to be. Amira has a gift. Let her use it."

"I want Amira to have the gifts of marriage
and children. Her desires are pushing these away."

Old Anwar says,
"Stubborn woman, your close-mindedness
is pushing away Amira's brilliance."

I pull my *toob*'s scarf
firm at my ears.
I do not want to hear this fighting.

I come inside
to find my mother and teacher
each gripping an end
of my tablet.

The soaked pallet sheet drips,
trickling droplets onto my toes.

Muma snaps,
"Amira, I found *this* tucked beneath your pallet."

She tugs at my yellow paper.
Old Anwar will not let go.

"This impractical man has told me about
your lessons."

Old Anwar's gaze cuts to mine.
His chest rises and falls
with hard breaths.

My mother, so angry,
so fevered with fear.

But her eyes are filled with curiosity,
glimpsing the words and pictures
that fill my pages.

OPINIONS

Muma lets go of my paper,
leaves it in Old Anwar's clenched fingers.
"You are fools," she says. "Both of you."

Muma takes the dripping sheet from me.
"And now, foolish girl, you are wasting water."

She slides past me to go outside,
where I hear her sloshing the fabric
in its cleaning basin.

I speak more quiet than a whisper.
I ask Old Anwar,
"Did you tell her my wish?"

He shakes his head.

With no sound at all,
I mouth another question,
a worry that is clamping
down tight.

My pencil?

Old Anwar reaches into the folds of his *jallabiya.*

He says,
"Your mother has many opinions
about me, Amira, but I am not a fool."

MUMA BLOOMING

Muma and I,
quiet.

Poking at the cook's fire,
a crackling splash of sparks.

Rubber-twig kindling
burns slowly,
holds heat,
smolders to make
a smoky curtain,
thick between us.

Our poking sticks are sturdy.
Mine starts a dance on the dirt.

Sweesh...swoosh!

Muma watches,
eyebrows puckered,
waiting to see what my stick will do.
She tilts her head.

Sweesh...swoosh!
Sweesh...swoosh!

I shape two faces.

Dot-dot eyes.
Sickle-sickle noses.

Muma asks,
"Who are *they*?"

I say,
"Me and you."

Muma's stick
starts to scrape
at the dirt.
Timidly at first,
but still scratch-scratching.

Does her stick want to dance?

Slowly, slowly
my mother's stick begins
its own loose shapes,
its own *sweesh-swoosh*.

Her stick-dance takes over.
Bold rhythm!

A curly-headed hibiscus
blooms quick
from the tip
of Muma's stick.

Sweeessssh...swooooossh!
Sweeessssh...swooooossh!

She draws
a wreath
that enfolds
my stick-shaped faces.

A ruffle-hug frame,
surrounding Muma and me.

Muma's eyes fill with
discovery.

Just days after deeming me a fool,
my mother
has found a treasure
she didn't know was hidden.

Muma, good for you.
Good for you, Muma.

She asks, "May I add to your faces?"

I say, "*Ya,* Muma. *Ya!*"

Her stick-dance rejoices.
Two upturned curves
bring stick-drawn smiles!

The fire's rubber-twig smoke
drifts off into night's breezes,
clears the curtain,
revealing us.

TALKING TO SAYIDDA MOON

She is full tonight,
bright.

A lighted ball
flaunting plump abundance,
high
in a so-black sky.

She watches down
on all of Kalma
while everyone sleeps,
but me.

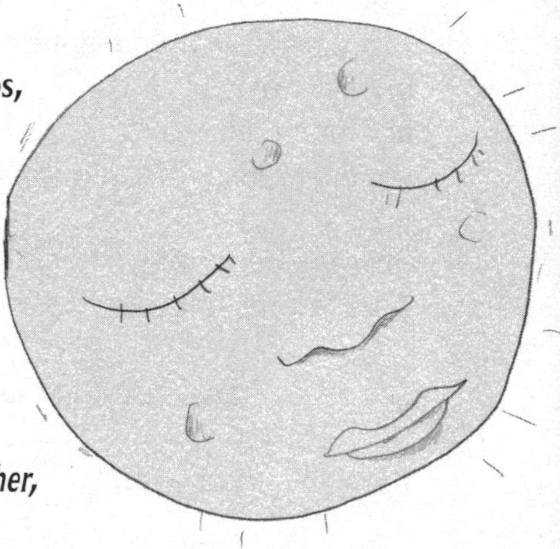

I speak
to her in a prayer,
a plea
for guidance.

Sayidda Moon,
I have a very sad mother,
who loves me,
and is trying to see me.
But mostly,
Muma's strong beliefs
are as blinding as a sun
that makes her squint at new ideas.

Sayidda Moon,
I have a wish big enough to fill ten gallon jugs.

Sayidda Moon,
my wish is a hymn that sifts
through my soul's
driest parts, cooling me.

Sayidda Moon,
I want to be a hedgehog,
slipping off to school.

What should I do?

Sayidda Moon does a slow roll,
disappears behind
a cloud-screen.

I watch.
I wait.

Soon, without noisy coaxing,
Sayidda Moon reemerges,
splashing milk.

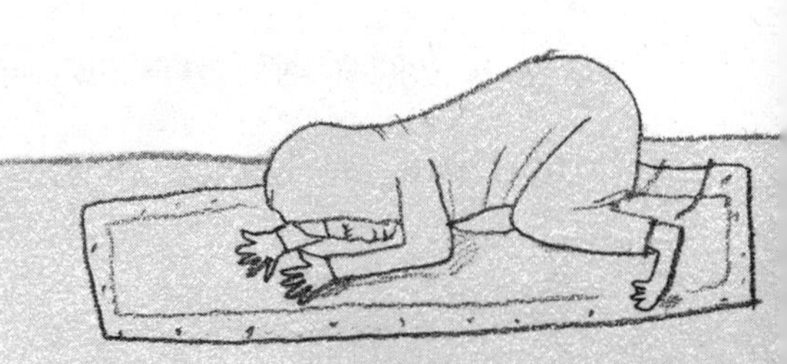

POSSIBILITIES

If I flee
for Nyala,
I could be eaten
to pieces
by
mosquitoes,
scorpions,
the Janjaweed.

If I run,
the double-sided dilemma
of Kalma's wolf
could bite me back
to this land
of Sudanese flowers
and rice-bag
domes.

Warnings
siren in my mind:

The one who leaves does not return.

And:

It is dangerous beyond this place.

I refuse to let these linger.

Quickly, I try to replace doubt
with a hope-bell
whose sound is just as loud.

If I escape Kalma's boundaries,
what else *is possible?*

DIRECTIONS

Today Old Anwar introduces
readings from the Koran,
Islam's holy text.

He has no book,
no pages,
no scroll to show me.

Old Anwar,
he just knows
what he knows
about what he calls "the soul's teachings."

The Koran's wisdom flows from
Old Anwar.

"Allah is the light," he says.

I ask,
"How do you find Allah's light?"

Old Anwar says,
"Take the path that shines brightest."

SUDANESE FLOWERS, REBORN

With my pencil,
I turn trash bags
into pretty
petaled
blossoms,
stemming from
fences,
adorned
with *sparrow*
scrollwork.

Ruby ornaments
decorate
my yellow tablet's
blue-line fences.

BURSTING

Dando's tomatoes.

Pride-fruits
filled
with seeds of possibility.

My red pencil's color
as ripe with promise
as these bursting-good
memories.

A new funny-bug letter.

A new word.

Writing it makes me smile.

T
Tomato

I AM

I am the red pencil!

Celebrating
the making
of marks that come from a place
known to me only when I let myself play.

And dream.

I am the line.

The joy-dance
that leaps from my tip.

I am the swirl.

The girl with the *sparrow*
who knows
how to draw,
how to write.

Letters,
faces,
hedgehogs,
tomatoes.

Memories.

No rules to this fun,
no laws,
only freedom.

UP, UP, ME

I let go,
scrawl,
climb,
scribble.

Spread every bit of my
simple,
quiet
point-power.

The red pencil is me.

THIRST RETURNS

For the first time,
I see that girl,
not much older than me,
has a melon belly.

Soon she will bear the child of her smoking husband.
Soon she will be forced to collect her family's ration
from the water giver's tight fist,
while her rude husband blows his smoke
too close to their newborn child.

I look and look at the girl.
Her expression is empty.

Will the girl's baby fill her with joy,
or has her life become a drained basin?

Seeing her
makes me very thirsty.

FLY OR DIE

My Fanta flute
is filled with flies.

A family,
glossy wings
flattened against their backs.

Crawling at the bottle's bottom,
jumbled,
confused.

They try to climb,
but instead bump the sides
of the glass canal,
frantic,
folding in on one another.

I shout,
"Look up—a hole!"

But the buzzing bunch
is blinded by their own frenzy.

I shout,
"Do you see the open *O*?
Do you see the escape?"

Maybe they know there's a way out,
but are too frightened by the possibility.

This fly family
feels at home in their clammy Fanta-land.

But they can't stay inside forever,
crowding,
swarming,
breathing stale Fanta air.

They must fly or die.

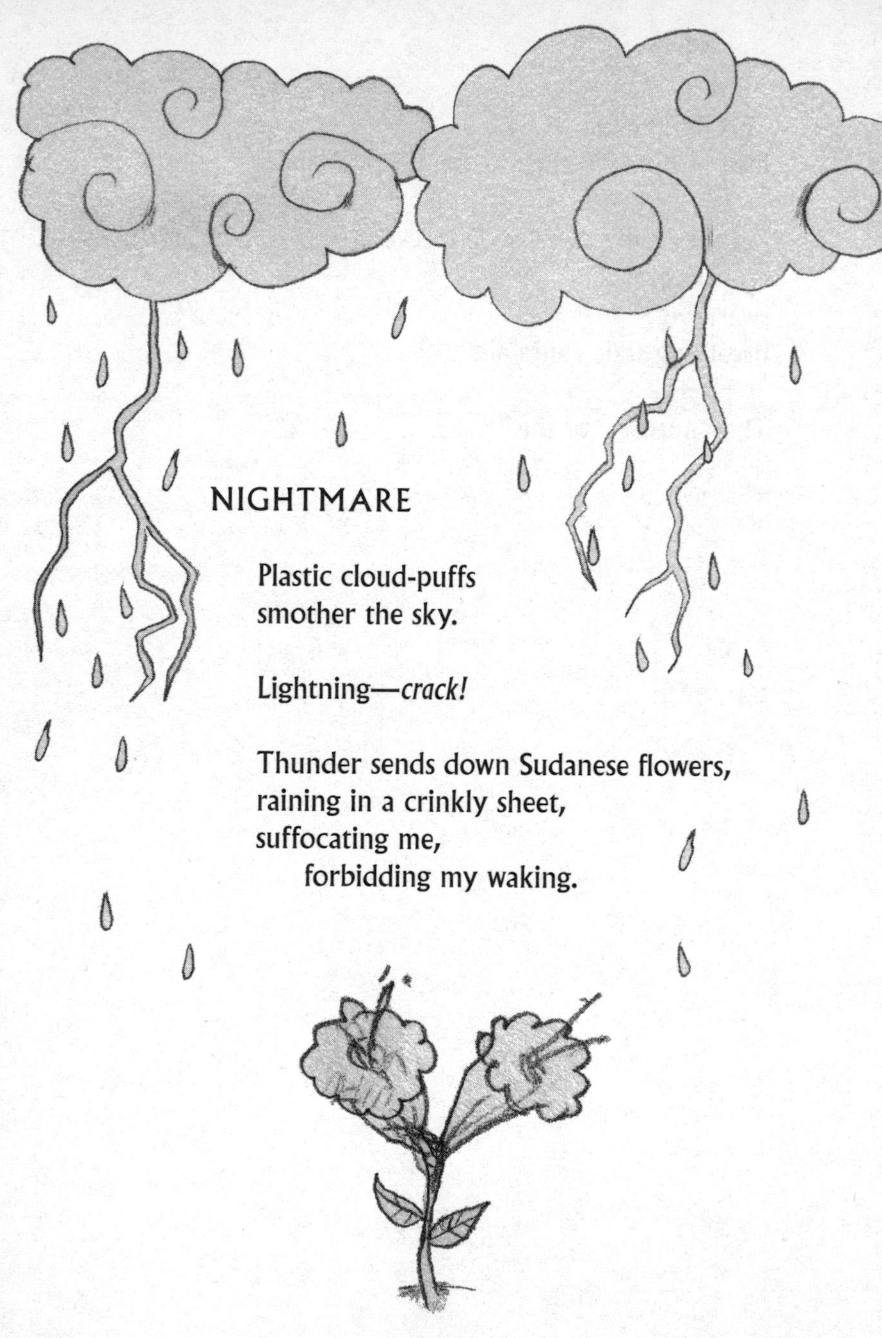

NIGHTMARE

Plastic cloud-puffs
smother the sky.

Lightning—*crack!*

Thunder sends down Sudanese flowers,
raining in a crinkly sheet,
suffocating me,
    forbidding my waking.

DUMB DONKEY

"You, girl!"

I'm on my way to our hut
to help Muma with evening chores.

There is sweeping to do,
then prayers.

He's gruff, calling to me,
insisting,
"Come, help carry!"

It's the rude husband of the
melon-bellied girl.

He's balancing a bundle of
thatch, as big as an ox,
a rolled mat,
a tin pail,
a half-open burlap sack,
leaking beans.

The mat is slipping.
Shards of thatch fall loose from
the twine cinched at its middle.

A burning cigarette
droops from the man's gray lips,
looking like a dead worm.

"You—I need help!"

Where is his wife?
No place nearby that I can see.

Perhaps she is awaiting his arrival,
watching from tattered slits
in the rice-bag walls of their home.

There are men about,
and plenty of boys.

They could help him.
But he calls only to me.

I don't look in his direction.
I don't let him know that I hear him.
I pretend to be as clueless as a dumb donkey.

LOOMING

Me,
today.

Me,
tomorrow.

Me,
ten moons come,
forty moons gone.

Me,
after hundreds of suns
have watched nothing new grow.

Me,
eyes hollow stains of waste,
staring nowhere.

Me,
here,
will become a Sudanese flower,
stuck to thorny fences,
      stunted.

This is an ugly picture.
I want to erase it.

CNN DAYDREAM

The flicker box bursts its door wide open,
inviting me to a CNN party.

Amira, welcome!

I'm wearing a Gad School *toob.*
I'm chanting a song about funny-bug letters.

A...B...C...D...
L...M...N...
O...P...
X...
Y...Z...

Halima and me.
And the letters, too.

Playing, dancing,
learning-words fun.

This dream.
A glory-sun,
splashing!

PROMISES

I drape Leila
in a secret
and a promise.

I tell her
birds can't fly in Kalma's cage.

I tell her
I must go.

I tell her
not to tell anyone.

Leila listens,
her eyes staying on mine.

I dress my sister
in my birthday *toob*.
The billowy blue sheath
is too big,
but Leila refuses to let its spilling cotton
swallow her.

"I will fill it," she says,
cinching its fabric,
sliding back the head drape
that slopes past her nose,
securing the sheer cloth closer to her ears.

"It fits you already," I say.

SISTER-TO-SISTER

Leila's eyes come back to mine.
She's waiting for me to tell more.

So I do.

I explain my wish,
and how I hope to grant it:

Nyala.
The Gad School.

Leila pays close attention.
She's grimacing.

"How can you just leave us, Amira?
You are being a silly lizard."

Leila starts to whimper,
but instead
works harder to keep her *toob* secure.

"I'll return, Leila," I say.

"I'll come back
to teach
what I learn."

I promise Leila
I will bring books
and pencils, pencils, pencils.

And a path to a chance
for her,
Gamal,
the melon-bellied girl,
and every child born
behind rice-bag walls.

Leila's gaze pulls in my promises,
sweet,
like Fanta.

I give her a kiss,
a gentle peckle-peck
to each side of her small,
wide face.

Sun has dried the brown
on Leila's cheeks and neck.

But it hasn't dulled the expectation
growing in her eyes.

GOOD-BYE GIFTS

Left behind.

My Fanta flute,
washed clean,
for Gamal.

For Old Anwar,
my plump tomato memory,
drawn by me
with a *T*.

For Muma,
my red pencil and tablet,
and a page filled simply
with my favorite shape.

My favorite funny-bug letter,
rolling in a row:

O O O

Open.
Unbroken.
Eternal.

NOW

Dusk.

The sun,
setting low,
a sliced-open yam
dipped in orange Fanta,
smiling sweet.

A birdcall
echoes from far off.

I listen.

It comes again
with a friend,
and swells to greet the evening.

An urgent whisper
spills.

Now, Amira!

I gather dried beans to eat.

I take a small tin of sesame oil
to keep free of mosquitoes.

I walk,
swift,
sure,
silently.

The Fanta sun dips
to become a low-hanging globe
blurring the horizon.

I do as I'm taught from the Koran.
I follow Allah's light.

Night is coming fast.

Old Anwar is away
in search of firewood.

Muma, Leila, and Gamal
have gone ahead
to Kalma's central tent for evening prayers.

They expect I will join them.

At this moment,
there are no watchful eyes to stop me.

No questions about where I am,
or where I'm going.

And—*ya!*—I *do* go.

ITCHY DOUBT

It pinches,
presses down hard,
twists me up,
tips me off-balance.

It is heavy,
but makes me light-headed,
like playing dizzy donkey.

It's as bothersome as needle noses.

Leave me alone!

But it won't let up.
It bites me while I flee.

Itchy doubt.

DANDO BRIGHT!

As itchy doubt prickles my skin,
a sudden moon shadow,
silver-white,
paints a shape
on the dark ground ahead,
lighting it.

Am I truly seeing
what I am seeing?

Bright
guidance!

Dando's silhouette!

My feet follow fast.

PRAY, WAIT

I walk—racing.

Past dome dwellings,
past Sudanese flowers,
my determined sandals tamping down
smelly dirt.

My *toob*
picks up the little breeze
made by my hurried steps.

Ahead I see the intake gate.
Tonight there are *two* Safari Suits,
both men guarding.

I yield.

One Safari Suit has lit the wick
on his nighttime lantern.

Why this man must wear green-dark glasses
after the sun has set,
I do not understand.

But it's better this way.
With shaded eyes,
he can see less of me.

The other Safari Suit stretches,
yawns.

My eye is on the chain-link fence behind
and to the side of them,
its gate an open sliver.

I hold back.
Pray.
Wait.

HEDGEHOG ESCAPE

At the intake station,
there is a table.

On its top rests a single bottle of Fanta.
Safari Suit with the green-dark glasses takes a swig,
sets down the drink.

His Safari Suit partner is quick
to pick up where his friend
left off.

He snaps up the bottle,
guzzles.

I can't hear what the two men say,
but right away I see
they're squabbling
over Fanta.

These grown-up men
wrestle the bottle's neck,
each struggling to make the soda their own.

The Fanta falls to the dirt.
Both Safari Suits lunge,
grapple,
shove to get that glass vessel,
now spilling its insides.

I slide behind
the fighting,
foolish men.

Slip through the intake gate.

Hedgehog escape!

QUICKENED

All of me beats
fast,
blood pumping,
heart sputtering,
quickened breaths.

I'm toe-deep in thick dirt.

It's soft,
inviting me to walk,
walk, walk.

From here,
I don't know
where Nyala is,
or which way to go.

Sayidda Moon is out,
a half-circle slice,
encrusting night's black *toob*.

I follow the Koran's teachings.
Take the path that shines brightest.

I move in the direction of *Sayidda* Moon's
gleaming light.

I'm not far when I hear rustling
and creaking,
and feet coming up behind me!

A lantern's hot splash of light
floods at my back.

The creaking stops,
but not the heavy steps.

I start to run.
The lamplight follows fast
in back of me,
approaching.

I run and run
and *run*.

The lamplight spreads wide,
catching up,
spewing a shadow.

Two solid hands pounce
on my shoulders.

"Amira!"

THE TRUTH

"Child! Have you been stripped
of all that is sensible?"

It's Old Anwar,
holding a lantern near his chin.

He looks angry.

His tone is sharp,
but his eyes, soft.

"What has possessed you, Amira?
It is not safe out here for a girl
traveling alone after dark.
Where, in the name of Allah, are you going?"

I can't lie to Old Anwar.
I answer simply and honestly.

"I have left Kalma for good.
I'm walking to Nyala.
I want to attend the Gad School."

Gently, Old Anwar says,
"Do you have any idea how to get to Nyala?"

I shake my head.

"I'm following the Koran's guidance,
taking the path *Sayidda* Moon has shown me."

Old Anwar speaks quietly.
He will not let me escape his gaze.
"Even with light on your path,
how can you walk to a place you do not know?"

My breathing has slowed,
but I now feel as though I will cry.

Old Anwar says,
"You cannot walk alone."

Hard wanting stomps at my throat.
I've come this far.
I don't want to go back.
I *do* cry now.

WE

I clamp both hands over my eyes.
Old Anwar sets his lantern
next to my feet.

He steps quickly away,
returns with his wheelbarrow,
hinges moaning.

He unloads the piled firewood,
dumps it right where we're standing.

"Get in," he says firmly.

I gather the fabric of my *toob*,
secure myself
in the dented well.
The wheelbarrow squeaks.

I give Old Anwar
my tin of sesame oil.

He spills a small river into his
palm,
slathers those thirsty hinges,
then my cheeks
and nose,
and backs of hands.

Old Anwar douses himself with the oil.

He offers me his lantern,
lifts the wooden handles.

The wheelbarrow tips.

Old Anwar says,
"Hold on."

FLIGHT

Morning.

Me,
rising
high,
wings
spread.

Casting a stippled shadow
over Kalma,
I fly off.

Sparrow child.

My beak,
my gaze,
straight,
not once looking down.

The rustling
of Sudanese flowers
fades
as I escape.

Trailing
        tail feathers.

What else is possible?

I am.

AUTHOR'S NOTE

Land of the Fur

The Darfur conflict unfolded in early 2003 in the western region of Sudan, a country in northeast Africa. The conflict sprung from an ongoing civil war. Fighting escalated when the Sudanese Liberation Army and the Justice and Equality Movement accused the government of Sudan of neglecting Darfur both politically and economically. As a result, the two armed movements declared war against the central government. The government relied on the Janjaweed, an ethnically based militia composed mainly of Arab groups, to fight the rebellion.

The largest tribal group in Darfur is that of the Fur people. Darfur, which means "land of the Fur," has suffered as warring groups fight over land and animal-grazing rights between nomadic Arabs and Fur farmers. Because of the staggering number of human casualties, the United States government describes what has happened in Darfur as genocide. Since 2003, at least 300,000 people have been killed and more than 2.5 million have been displaced inside Sudan and elsewhere.

These people have been uprooted from their homes, which were bombed or burned in brutal raids by the Janjaweed militia. In the aftermath of military slaughter, they have been forced to flee in search of safety. Many families travel great distances to reach one of several relocation camps throughout Sudan and Chad, a neighboring country. When a family sets out from their village, they often don't know where they're going, exactly. When they flee, their course is determined by what routes appear to be the safest, those free of potential attacks. To ensure they will not be seen, they travel mostly at night, hoping to get to the safety of a displacement camp.

While the refugee camps provide a haven, they are often overrun with people living among squalid conditions.

Kalma Camp, located in South Darfur, was considered one of the largest refugee centers as the conflict grew. At its peak, it accommodated nearly 90,000 residents. Those living in Kalma have very little hope of ever returning to their homes.

Finding Hope

When I first learned of the struggles unfolding in Darfur and Sudan, my heart broke. As the crisis worsened, I felt compelled to present the ugly effects of war to young readers in a way that could help them understand their impact. That is how *The Red Pencil* began.

Although I have traveled through several parts of Africa, conducted extensive research for this novel, and consulted with several experts, I am not an expert on the crisis in Darfur. As a novelist, I felt it vital to write a book that speaks to the human condition in times of war and to present this information in a way that is accessible to young readers. This story has been heavily vetted and fact-checked. Any errors or omissions are unintended. My hope is that I've written a book that is true in its soul and that speaks to the indomitable spirit of a people.

The Red Pencil is a work of fiction inspired by several accounts that I read about children growing up inside an unthinkable reality.

Young people witnessed horrific acts of war. With their families and surviving neighbors, they fled to refugee camps in search of safety.

The Red Pencil's illustrated poems follow one child's journey through grief and possibility. Part novel, part sketchbook, this story celebrates the power of creativity, and the way that art can help us heal. It is intended to be a book about hope, the resilience of the human spirit in the wake of devastating circumstances, and how artistic expression can transcend the wounds of war. I wrote this novel with a weeping heart. The use of prose poems to tell Amira's story is deliberate. I found that verse could be a means of insulating young readers from the tragic realities of genocide and could offer a way to make the horrors of war easier to comprehend.

Poetry also encourages young readers to express their own emotions and troubles, and to find comfort in the most upsetting circumstances.

According to LitWorld, a global literacy advocacy organization, 523 million girls and women worldwide cannot read or write. This is especially true in developing nations. In Darfur, the illiteracy rate among girls is alarmingly high. Darfurian schools cost money that each family must pay if they want their children to attend. Many families do not have the funds for education. Girls are often forced to stay out of school to help with household tasks and farming chores. Also, in rural areas, education for girls can be seen as a threat to traditional values. Girls are often expected to marry young and work on their family land, herding animals and tending the home.

Fortunately, teachers and international aid groups are working to increase educational opportunities for girls, especially those in cities, small villages, and safety camps.

In 2004, when most of this story is set, Kalma was just beginning to entertain the idea of creating a school. There were fledgling attempts, but because the war was new and tensions were high, people were still trying to determine what would happen after the initial crisis. At that time, within Kalma's confines, school was not a priority. Also, families still clung to traditional values, which discouraged educational access for girl children.

On the dusty outskirts of Nyala, South Darfur's largest town, there is a school called Qud al Haboob, also referred to as Gad al Haboob. This school is known for its rare distinction—the sizable population of girls who attend. In 2012, among the school's 186 students, 98 were girls. For the sake of this novel, I've modified the school's name to Gad Primary School to avoid confusion with the story's references to the *haboob* sandstorms that sweep across the Sudan region.

It is not fully known how the Qud al Haboob got its name. Some believe it was named for its location in the region, where the *haboob* storms are prevalent.

The vignettes that make up this novel were inspired by personal accounts, interviews, transcribed narratives, and news stories.

As part of my research for *The Red Pencil*, I spent countless hours interviewing individuals who have lived through the Darfur conflict, and also workers who have traveled into refugee camps providing aid to families and children.

These courageous people were eager to share their stories with me, in the hope that *The Red Pencil* could be a means by which young readers can understand the shocking complexity of Darfur's struggle and the tragedies and triumphs of those who have survived.

In addition to recounting details about the war, these men and women shared colorful stories of village life, tribal customs, local agriculture, and farming practices. Several bits of detail about conditions in Darfur and Sudan in 2004 came from these conversations. *Dando* and *Muma* are Amira's own terms of endearment for her parents. The tribal beliefs about calling the moon, and the moon's showing power, are based on my interviews with Darfurian refugees. So are the references to animal habits, life in a refugee camp, clothing, and weather patterns.

Many brave people have spoken out against the struggles in Darfur. Governments are working to end the war. But the atrocities continue. Children and their families still suffer.

The Red Pencil is written to honor them.

ACKNOWLEDGMENTS

It is with great thanks that I extend gratitude to many who opened their homes, schools, and memories to help make this book's story authentic.

Thanks to Dr. Ali B. Ali-Dinar, associate director of the University of Pennsylvania African Studies Center, for his valuable remarks on the manuscript.

Heartfelt thanks to Abdalmageed S. Haroun, founder and executive director of the Human Rights and Advocacy Network for Democracy (HAND), whose personal journey from Darfur to the United States illuminates the passages found in this book.

Abdalmageed S. Haroun and Andrea Davis Pinkney celebrate the power of red pencils.

I extend gratitude to Nisrin Elamin, whose work with Global Kids, the National Youth Leadership Council, and Girfina, a Sudanese nonviolent resistance movement—and her tireless efforts on behalf of young people and displaced individuals living in Sudan's refugee camps—served as inspiration for Amira's story.

Appreciation goes to Carol Sakoian, vice president, Scholastic International, and a member of the Council on Foreign Relations, for her in-depth understanding of Africa's literacy development and school systems. I am grateful to workers from the United Nations Development Programme—Bruno Lemarquis for putting me in touch with those who are on the front lines striving to improve conditions in Darfur and Sudan, and Asmaa Shalabi, program specialist in the United Nations Development Programme Bureau of Crisis Prevention and Recovery, for her insights and knowledge about displaced families. Thank you, Jennifer Vilaga, for your extensive research help and fact-checking.

Special thanks to Mark Doty and Courtney Nuzum Jiménez, middle school codirectors at the Mary McDowell Friends School, and teachers Beverly Wind and Erica Fry for sharing their current-events curriculum about Darfur and Sudan and for offering helpful suggestions and guidance on ways to present this information to young readers.

Thank you, editors Liza Baker, Alvina Ling, and Allison Moore, whose wise editorial guidance helped shape this book's narrative. Thank you, Rebecca Sherman, my agent and guide. Artist and visionary Shane Evans, your drawings have brought this story to incredible visual life. Liz Casal, your design brilliance has beautifully shaped the novel's presentation.

And finally, to Brian, thank you for loving me.

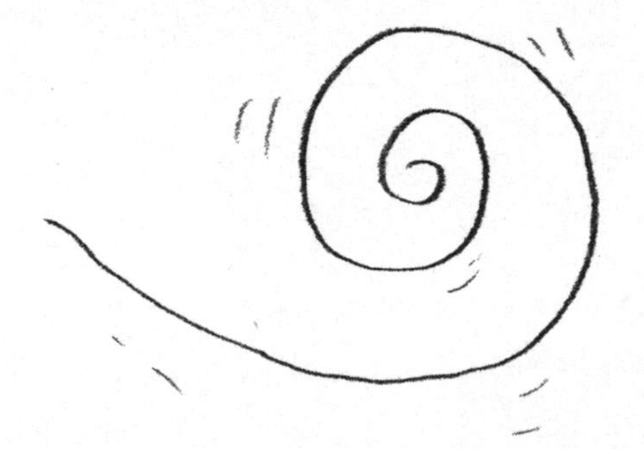

GLOSSARY/PRONUNCIATION GUIDE

There are many tribal languages spoken throughout Sudan and in Darfur. Arabic is the most common and widely used language. These are some of the traditional Arabic words that appear in this book, along with their definitions and phonetic pronunciations.

aakh (ahk)—ouch.

Allah (ah-LAH)—the Arabic word used for God primarily by people who practice Islam.

goz (gahz)—the sandy soil that covers the hills and plains of Darfur.

haboob (hah-BOHB)—a violent dust storm, which occurs in Sudan. The storm produces a wall of sand and clay that can temporarily reduce visibility.

jallabiya (jah-LAH-bee-yah)—a long robe-like garment worn by men and boys. Also referred to as *jalabiya*, *jalabbiya*, or *galabiyya*.

Koran (kor-AHN)—the religious text of Islam. Muslims believe the Koran is the word of God. Some regard the Koran as the most sacred literature in the Arabic language.

Sayidda (sie-ee-dah)—Lady.

shukran (shoo-krahn)—an expression of gratitude. "Thank you."

tarha (tar-HAH)—a rectangular piece of cloth worn by a girl as a head scarf; also worn by an older woman under the *toob*.

toob (tohb)—a sari-like long piece of fabric worn by a Sudanese woman as an outer garment to wrap her whole body. Also referred to as *tobe* or *tawb*.

ya (yah)—an affirmation, equivalent to "yeah." This term is not proper Arabic. It is a colloquialism.

CHARACTER/LOCATION PRONUNCIATIONS

Amira (ah-MEER-ah)
Dando (DAHN-doh)
Darfur (dar-FUR)
Farha (far-haah)
Gamal (gah-MAHL)
Halima (hah-lee-mah)
Janjaweed (jan-jah-weed) Also referred to as Janjawid.
Kalma (kel-mah)
Khartoum (kar-toom)
Leila (lay-lah)
Miss Sabine (sib-EEN)
Muma (MOO-mah)
Nali (NAH-lee)
Nyala (nie-AH-lah)
Old Anwar (AHN-ware)
Salma (sahl-mah)

IMPORTANT TERMS THAT APPEAR IN THIS BOOK

armed—carrying a weapon.

civil war—a conflict in which one group of people in a country opposes another.

displaced—forced to leave home or a homeland.

displaced people's camps—places where people go to find safety in the midst of war after fleeing their homes; also referred to as relocation camps and refugee camps.

genocide—the killing of a large group of people, often from a particular race or culture.

militia—a group of regular citizens who are not soldiers, but who have been enlisted to help the army fight.

nomads—people who don't have a home base who wander in search of food, water, and shelter.

persecution—the harassment or punishment of people because of their beliefs.

rebellion—the act of going against authority, often in a violent way.

renegade—a person who deserts the beliefs of his or her religion or government, sometimes in an illegal way.

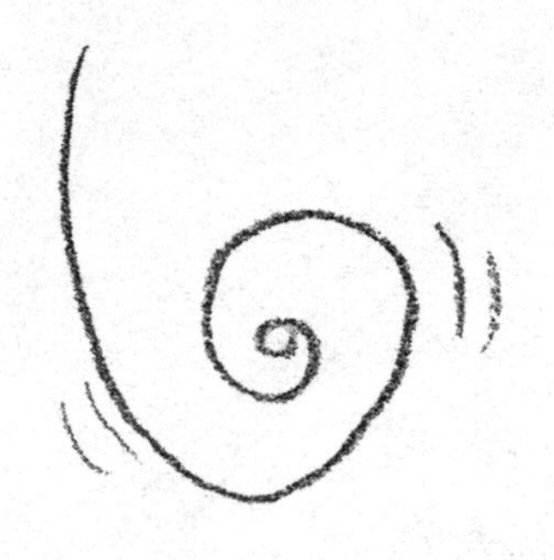

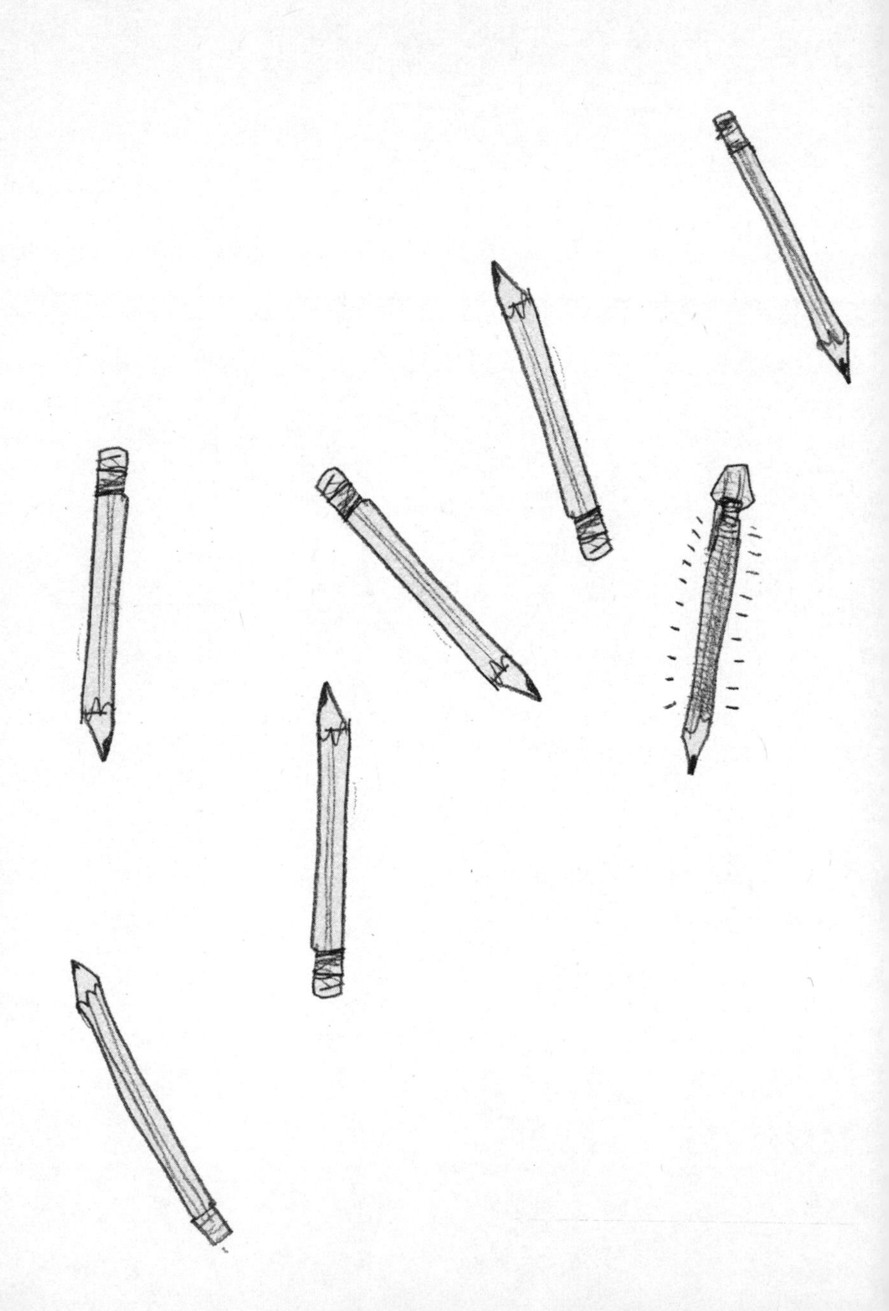

DISCUSSION GUIDE

Part 1

1. Amira's birthday is an important family occasion. What is so special about her twelfth birthday? What do her parents, Dando and Muma, say about her birthday? What do their words tell you about Amira?

2. Amira's best friend, Halima, and her family leave the village and move to Nyala, a bustling city. Halima's father is searching for opportunity. What does he expect to find in the city? Why, do you think, is Amira's family not moving to the city?

3. Amira says that Halima's parents "are modern people, / not stifled by tradition." What are the differences between the modern and traditional Sudanese ways of life? Which does Amira prefer? Why?

4. Dando uses words like *persecution*, *rebellion*, and *genocide* to describe war. Muma uses words like *armed*, *militia*, *bandits*, and *renegades* to describe the Janjaweed. How are these words alike and different?

5. The moon appears throughout the story as a greatly influential symbol. Explain why *Sayidda* Moon is such an important force in Amira's village. What is the tradition of waking the moon?

6. On the night that Leila, Amira's sister, was born, how did the family know she would be "different"? How did the family react when they saw her? In your opinion, why did they react that way?

7. Despite their loving relationship, Amira and her mother clash in an ongoing difference of opinion. What subjects do they disagree on? In your opinion, why does Amira's mother feel the way she does? Why does Amira feel the opposite?

8. A significant part of Sudanese life and culture is *goz*. What does Amira mean when she refers to *goz* as Darfur's great blanket? Why does she have such deep reverence for it?

9. Amira describes the way she draws in the following manner:

   My hand

   and my twig

   and my *sparrow*

   do the dance

   on the sand.

   Why does she use these words? What does *sparrow* mean in this context? What words would you use to describe your own drawing?

10. Dando and Amira share a game called "What Else Is Possible?" Why is it a favorite game for both of them? How do you think they feel when they play this game?

11. Old Anwar and Dando agree that Amira should learn to read. However, they face the objection of Amira's mother. What arguments would you offer to persuade her to agree with them?

12. Amira notices "a strange shadow / in people's eyes." How does she respond when she looks at the faces of the villagers? What is meant by "eyes tell / what is inside"?

13. In the wake of a horrific raid by the Janjaweed, the villagers must flee the safety and security of their homes. Describe their experiences during the journey to Kalma in terms of their emotional states and physical challenges.

Part 2

1. The refugees finally arrive at Kalma. What are Amira's impressions of her new home? How do they compare to the farm life she left behind?

2. Amira, her mother, Leila, and Gamal are greatly affected by the outcome of the raid. How does each cope with grief in the aftermath? How do their behaviors change?

3. Amira has never seen a television before. What role does the "flicker box" play in the story? How does Amira react to it? What new meaning does it have for her when she likens it to the displacement camp?

4. Miss Sabine from Sudan Relief visits Kalma to give the children pencils and paper. She makes a special gift to Amira. Why, do you think, did she give the red pencil to Amira? How does Amira compare it to the twig she used in the village?

5. When Amira shows her red pencil to Old Anwar, he responds, "It suits you.... / Such a bold color. Strong." After she shares her drawings, he looks closely and says, "Healing." What is the message he is conveying to her?

6. Amira very much wants to learn to read. Old Anwar offers to teach Amira to read in secret, by lantern at night, and not tell Muma. Do you think this is a good idea? Why or why not? How do you think Muma will react when she learns of this plan?

7. Amira is grateful to Old Anwar for teaching her to read, but her wish is to

    have lessons

    in a real school,

    with other girls,

    with Halima.

   Knowing that the family has no money to send her to school, she shares her feelings anyway. Should she have told Old Anwar about her wish? Why or why not?

8. There were no hedgehogs on Amira's village farm. Why is she so fascinated with this unfamiliar creature? Why does she tell *Sayidda* Moon that her big wish is to be "a hedgehog, / slipping off to school"?

9. Amira has made her decision. She is leaving to go to Nyala to attend the Gad School. However, she has "itchy doubt." Why, do you believe, is she so apprehensive? How does she manage to overcome these feelings?

10. The last verse of the story is titled "Flight." How does this word reflect the essence of the story? What other word could you use to describe a culminating theme?

THREE KIDS SHARE THE DREAMS OF A CHAMPION....

TURN THE PAGE FOR AN EXCERPT OF
BIRD IN A BOX!

ONE

SPEAKY

June 21, 1937

HIBERNIA

FOR CRYING OUT LOUD! SKIP GIBSON, YOU have done it again. You have turned *Happy* Hibernia into *Not*-Happy Hibernia.

How dare you interrupt *Swing Time at the Savoy* to announce the fight. Jeepers!

I'm as eager as anybody to see if Joe Louis wins, but that's a whole day away. It's bad enough that for months I've had to sneak-listen to the reverend's radio. And now that he's finally letting me enjoy my favorite program on the CBS Radio Network, you, Skip Gibson, have squashed it.

The truth is, if the reverend knew I was still thinking about singing—or *swinging*—at the Savoy, he'd lock me in the parish broom closet for a month. But that's Speaky's power. Speaky brings the Savoy to me and lets me dream. Even from the broom closet, I can escape to center stage, thanks to Speaky.

This all began early last summer when the parishioners at our church bought my daddy, the reverend, his brand-new Zenith radio. A gift to celebrate the church's fifth anniversary.

The reverend wasted no time getting to know his newfangled present. That's how Speaky got to be a member of our little family. My daddy even *named* his radio. *Speaky,* he calls it.

Daddy loves Speaky so much that he makes me dust the radio as part of my cleaning chores. Sometimes he watches to make sure I'm doing it right. "Bernie," he says, "give Speaky a rub with the polish, will you?" And there I am, pleasing Daddy, putting a shine to the top of Speaky, as if the radio were a bald prince getting a head wax.

Speaky is perched right next to the writing table the reverend keeps in the closed-off corner of the vestry, the private place where he writes his sermons. That cramped little space is no bigger than a bread bin, though the reverend makes it sound like it's some official office. He calls it his *sermon sanctuary.*

For the longest time, I was not allowed to listen to the reverend's radio. He said he was trying to protect my virtue. But I am no gullible piece of peanut brittle. I know it was more than that. The reverend was right in thinking the radio would get me to missing my mother, Pauline. When my mama left for New York City right after I was born, she hit the road with a heavy suitcase packed full with her big dream—to sing at the Savoy Ballroom, one of the swankiest nightspots in Harlem.

Some days I wish my mother had taken me with her. I guess there just wasn't enough room for me in her overstuffed luggage. But, oh, would I love something else to remember her by. All I know now of my mother is her name, Pauline—and, well, the music on the radio.

That's not much. Especially since I'm left here growing up with the reverend, who, most days, is as starched as the rice water I use to iron his shirt collars.

Sometimes it is no slice of pie being the daughter of the Reverend C. Elias Tyson, minister of the True Vine Baptist Church congregation.

Everybody *adores* the reverend. To his parishioners, he can do no wrong. But in the eyes of my daddy, there are some things that can never be right.

For instance, he knows I can outsing most folks, but my desire to be a big-city performer is bad news to the reverend. It riles him.

Hibernia Lee Tyson is not giving up, though. I'm going to take the dream my mother had for herself and make it come true for me.

Along with Ella Fitzgerald, Chick Webb, and Duke Ellington, someday I will call the Savoy my own. I may have to wait till I'm grown. But if the chance comes any sooner, I will jump on that chance faster than I land on a hopscotch square.

Don't let me admit any of this around the reverend. He has other notions for me. "Bernie Lee," he declares, "places like the Savoy are a hotbed of sinful activity. I believe you've been called to a more fruitful occupation. I feel strongly that you're meant to someday take over as the director of the True Vine Baptist choir."

I don't see anything sinful about singing in a ballroom. Time and time again, I have tried to tell the reverend that to deny me the opportunity to present my vocal abilities to a dance-floor crowd is to trap my God-given gifts under a butterfly net. To me, *that* is a sin.

Everyone in town knows that Hibernia Lee Tyson is going straight to the top. And you can bet your bottom dollar that I have the talent to take me there.

Other than the reverend, there are only two things holding me back. One is my age. I've just turned twelve, which is way too young for the Savoy. But I'm taller than most boys my age, and strong, too. And when I color my cheeks with face powder and use NuNile pomade to smooth my hair, I can pass for being a grown-up lady with real singing experience.

The other thing getting in my way to fame is my stubby fingernails, which I have bitten to the quick. You can't be a big star without nice nails. People love to get singers to sign their cocktail napkins after each show. But who wants an autograph by somebody with fingertips that look like half-eaten pig's knuckles?

The nail biting is a bad habit. No matter what, I can't stop. What makes it worse is all I try that *doesn't* work. I soak my fingers in pickle vinegar. I sit on my hands. I pretend my nails are covered with ants. None of this helps. For the life of me, I can't find a way to quit.

But there's one thing I know for certain. If I were out front at the Savoy Ballroom, I would show everybody that Hibernia Lee Tyson can roll out a tune sweet enough to bake. The world would have to wait for news about tomorrow's Joe Louis fight while Hibernia Lee lit up the airwaves with her song.

The truth is, though, I am no closer to Harlem or the

CBS Radio Network than I am to the moon. I am stuck here in slowpoke Elmira, New York, living upstairs from the True Vine Baptist Church with the Reverend C. Elias Tyson and Speaky, his radio.

Now Skip, don't get me wrong—I'm truly rooting for Joe. So is everybody I know. But *Not*-Happy Hibernia will turn back into *Happy* Hibernia by listening to *Swing Time at the Savoy.* Without interruptions.

But, all right. Seeing as tomorrow is Joe's big night, I guess all I can do is wait. And hope on Joe. And meanwhile, curse you, Skip Gibson, for stomping on my *Savoy*!

WiLLiE

MAMA, SHE TOLD ME TO LEAVE HOME. And it's just as well, I swear.

I couldn't stay unless Sampson hit the road for good. Sampson—what a lame excuse for a daddy. *Uh-huh,* that's Sampson. Nothin' but a sorry sack.

Even after all this time, Lila and the bleach man don't know I ain't like the rest of the orphans here at Mercy. That I got a mother and a father, and an address different from this place.

Thing is, though, the house where Mama and Sampson live ain't a real true home. Far as I can tell, you don't get burnt in a real home. Your daddy don't curse at your mama in a real home. In a real true home, your mama don't cry herself to sleep, and neither do you.

I get to thinking about Sampson and Mama every time I look at my Saint Christopher medal. And with Joe Louis about to step in the ring, I keep Saint Christopher close as ever. That medal's one of the only things I can say's all mine. Soon as I came here and unpacked my croker sack, Saint Christopher fell out on the floor, chain and all. Before then, the medal ain't seen much of the light of day.

I remember when Mama gave me Saint Christopher. Was my tenth birthday, near to three years back now. Mama, she'd put the little medal in a big box. Covered it all in brown paper. *Uh-huh,* Mama, she's good with making things special.

When I unwrapped the paper and opened the box, the medal was pushed under more crumpled bunches. Wasn't till I dug in the paper and found the small gift, that Mama explained, "It's a Saint Christopher medal. It protects travelers, especially young people, on their journeys."

I turned the little medal over and over in my hand. "Protecting people," I say. "*Uh-huh,* I like that."

Mama say, "And seeing as Saint Christopher was such an important man, I felt he should be housed in a mighty place. That's why I wrapped him so carefully for you, Willie."

When Mama slipped the medal's chain around my neck, Sampson, he started laughing. To him, the whole thing was just so funny. "Why you giving the boy a sissy thing like that?" He was sniffing when he say it. Talking like somethin' smells bad. "How's the boy ever gonna get respect if he's wearing a necklace?"

Sampson gave the medal a tug. Yanked my neck forward at the same time. "I guess you can use all the help you can get, Willie-bo." That's what Sampson called me, *Willie-bo*. He even liked turning my *name* into some kind of joke, funny only to him. That's why I couldn't never make myself call my father Pa. What kind of father laughs at his own son's name? *Uh-huh,* that's stupid, ain't it?

Sampson tugged on the medal again. I turned away from him quick. "When I was a boxer," Sampson say, "my coach told me to get a good-luck charm."

Half the time Sampson spoke, he started by saying, "When I was a boxer..."

But you ain't *no boxer now,* my mind's whispering.

"When I was a boxer, I should've listened to my coach and got me that good-luck charm. Maybe I never would've been saddled with a kid," Sampson say.

Mama, who was busy collecting the brown gift wrap, she flinched.

Sampson wouldn't let up. "Willie-bo, if it weren't for you, I'd still be boxing today—might even be a champ, instead of a outta-work bum with two mouths to feed and a sissy kid who likes wearing jewelry."

"Hush up, Sampson," Mama say. "That medal is a sign of strength."

With the way Sampson's talking about me being a sissy, I wouldn't let myself pay that medal a second thought. I stuffed that sissy thing way far back in my clothes crate, behind my moth-eaten socks.

I kept the brown paper the medal came in, though. *Uh-huh,* kept it. Later, after Sampson had went out drinking, I wrapped the paper around each of my fists, and did me a pair of play boxing gloves. I remember thinkin', *Scrap Sampson. Maybe someday* I *can be a champ.*

Them gloves was big brown slammers, just like Joe's. Paper dukes that made me feel like a boxing king. Made me wish I had a roaring right fist same like Joe Louis's so's I could knock Sampson out in one punch and leave him wishing he never do mess with Mama or me.

That same night, Mama told me what to do with my Saint Christopher medal. "Tell it your dreams."

Nowadays seems all I do is what Mama say. I whisper my secrets to Saint Christopher. And I wish on that medal every chance I get. Even if it *is* for sissies, it makes me feel good to do it.

I tell Saint Christopher that though I'm long gone from Sampson and Mama's house, I wish Sampson would fall headfirst off the face of the world. And I hope Mama will wake up one day and see Sampson for the sorry sack he is.

Today, since I'm hoping hard already, I won't pass up a chance to put in a good word for Joe.

My wish is short. But *uh-huh,* I mean it:

Let Joe win!

OTIS

WHAT DID THE TIE SAY TO THE HAT?

Why did the cookie go to the hospital?

What lays at the bottom of the ocean and shakes?

If riddles could march, tonight would be a riddle parade.

Here they come again. One riddle after another, in a happy line.

They sure are loud this time, a brass-and-drum band pounding inside my head. Playing on my mind, as if Daddy is here telling them himself.

Tonight I speak right to the riddles. I call their answers out into the dark. It's like waving at friends who smile when you see them passing.

"You go on ahead, and I'll just hang around!"

"Because it felt crummy!"

"A nervous wreck!"

That's when Lila comes running. The bleach man is with her. He tries to hush me. He tells Lila, "This boy needs to quiet down. He'll wake up the other children. Is he crazy?"

Lila says, "Riddles comfort Otis. It's just a dream he's having."

The bleach man is shaking his head.

Lila's hand is pressed to her cheek. She's watching me with kind eyes. Her skin is as pink as bubble gum, and smooth under its freckles.

There's nothing smooth or pink about Mr. Sneed. He's as pale as they come. A ghost has more color than he does. That's just one of the reasons I've nicknamed him the bleach man. Like bleach, Mr. Sneed is harsh. He strips the fun out of everything.

Lila's the opposite. She isn't mean. Nobody's bleached her heart.

It's not Lila's way to hush me up. If I ask her one of my riddles, she'll try to solve it, like the last time. She'll think of silly answers, and I'll feel better.

Before I can even stump Lila with one of my riddles, they come back fast.

What did the pig say on the hot summer day?

If you cross a snowball with a shark, what do you get?

Fingers grow on what kinds of trees?

As the riddle parade marches past, I yell out the answers with all I've got.

"I'm bacon!"

"Frostbite!"

"Palm trees!"

Soon the riddles are starting to go. The parade is moving off, and the riddles are gone. Gone till next time.

The thumping in my head is gone, too. But I'm hot as blazes. That's what happens when the riddles come into my dreams.

Lila lays the back of her hand to my forehead. "He's feverish," she tells the bleach man.

She takes a handkerchief from her sleeve. She dips it in the water basin, near to my cot, and wipes the little bit of wet from my face.

Lila knows I'm not crazy. Lila understands. I wish I could tell the bleach man that my mind's all my own. That even though it's near to a year, I'm still missing Ma and Daddy, is all. That sometimes Daddy's riddles still talk in my dreams, is all. Sometimes good dreams.

Sometimes bad ones. And sometimes, when I answer the riddles, I feel good.

That's all. That's all there is to it. Nothing crazy about me.

It's tomorrow's fight that's making me think of Daddy. It's people saying the press will have to eat their statement that boxing will never see a Negro champion. It's the wishing on Joe Louis that's bringing memories of Daddy and Ma back to me so strong.

Daddy believed in Joe. Joe was Daddy's hope.

Daddy believed in me, too. We made a deal, Daddy and me. We shook on a promise.

Now Joe is *my* hope. *My* promise.

If Daddy were here, he'd be putting his all on Joe. He'd be saying a different kind of riddle. He'd be asking a question that won't *be* a question come tomorrow.

What's set to explode while the whole world waits?

The Brown Bomber.

ALSO BY
ANDREA DAVIS PINKNEY

THEY DIDN'T NEED MENUS.
THEIR ORDER WAS SIMPLE.

A DOUGHNUT AND COFFEE,
WITH CREAM ON THE SIDE.

THEY WERE EACH BORN WITH THE GIFT OF GOSPEL.

MARTIN'S VOICE KEPT PEOPLE IN THEIR SEATS,
BUT ALSO SENT THEIR PRAISES SOARING.

MAHALIA'S VOICE WAS BRASS-AND-BUTTER—
STRONG AND SMOOTH AT THE SAME TIME.

AVAILABLE WHEREVER BOOKS ARE SOLD

CHRISTINE SIMMONS

ANDREA DAVIS PINKNEY is the *New York Times* bestselling and award-winning author of many books for children and young adults, including *Bird in a Box* and several collaborations with her husband, Brian Pinkney, among them *Sit-In*, *Martin & Mahalia*, and *Hand in Hand*, winner of the Coretta Scott King Award. She lives with her family in New York City.

GARY SPECTOR

SHANE W. EVANS is the illustrator of many books for young readers, including *Underground: Finding the Light to Freedom*, which won the Coretta Scott King Award, and *Nobody Gonna Turn Me 'Round*, which was nominated for the NAACP Image Award. His website is ShaneEvans.com.